ALEXANDER BELAYEV

THE AMPHIBIAN

Fredonia Books
Amsterdam. The Netherlands

The Amphibian

by
Alexander Belayev

ISBN: 1-58963-337-7

Copyright © 2001 by Fredonia Books

Reprinted from the original edition

Fredonia Books
Amsterdam, The Netherlands
http://www.fredoniabooks.com

CONTENTS

PART I

"The Sea-Devil" 7
Riding A Dolphin. 21
Zurita's Ill Luck 27
Dr. Salvator. 36
The Sick Granddaughter. 45
An Orchardful of Miracles . . 50
The Third Wall. 57
An Ambush 61
The Amphibian 68
A Day of Ichthyander's . . . 74
The Girl and the Stranger . . . 91
Ichthyander's Valet 95
In Town 104
Back in the Sea 110
Revenge Is Sweet. 118
The Impatience of Zurita 126
An Unpleasant Encounter 134
Fighting Octopuses. 140
A New Friend. 147

PART II

On the Way. 162
That's Him! 175
Full Speed Ahead! 184

The Extraordinary Prisoner 193
The Abandoned *Jellyfish* . . 205
The Sunken Ship 210

PART III

The Long-Lost Father 221
A Case Without Precedent 233
The Madman of Genius 241
Salvator's Explanation 248
In Prison 259
The Escape 276

"THE SEA-DEVIL"

T he close night of the Argentine midsummer came down on the sea. Stars pricked out in a sky that was a deep violet. The schooner *Jellyfish* lay quietly at anchor, with not a splash round her, not a creak on board. Ship and ocean seemed in deep slumber.

Half-naked pearl-divers sprawled on the deck. Worn out by the day's work under a parching sun they tossed and groaned and cried out in their nightmarish sleep. Their limbs would jerk and twitch; perhaps they were fighting off sharks–their deadly enemies. The hot windless weather of which they were having a spell made people so tired that they couldn't even hoist the boats on board at the end of a day's work. Not that it seemed necessary: nothing indicated a change in weather. So the boats were left afloat, made fast to the anchor chain. Nobody had thought of tightening the shrouds or sheeting home the jib which fluttered faintly at each stray whiff of wind. From bowsprit to taffrail the schooner was strewn with heaps of pearl shells, pieces of coral, lengths of diving cord, canvas sacks for putting shells in and empty barrels.

Against the mizzen-mast stood a big water barrel with an iron mug on a chain. The deck immediately round was stained dark with spilt water.

Every now and then a diver struggled up and staggered along, sleep-drunk, to the water barrel. Never opening his eyes he swallowed a mugful and dropped down anywhere on his way back, as if it were not water he had drunk but neat spirit. The divers were always thirsty. They went without morning meals, for underwater pressure made diving on a full stomach dangerous, so they worked without eating all through the day, till it grew too dark underwater. They had their meal before turning in—and that was of salt meat.

The Indian Baltasar, right hand of the schooner's owner Pedro Zurita, had the night watch.

In his time Baltasar had been known far and wide as an excellent pearl-diver. He could stay underwater for as much as a minute and a half or even two minutes which was about twice as long as an average diver.

"How did we do it? They knew how to train in my day and started early," Baltasar would say to the young divers.

"Just turned ten I was. My father took me to José, who owned a tender, for training. There were twelve of us, all kids like me. And this is the way he trained us. He'd throw a white pebble or shell into the water and order one of us to go and get it. And each time he found deeper and deeper places. If one of us had nothing to show for his diving José'd give him a lash or two of his whip and shove him overboard to try again. And it worked. Then he started to train us to keep longer times underwater. An experienced diver'd go down and make a basket or piece of netting fast to the anchor chain. Then down we went to untie the knots. And we weren't allowed to come up before all the knots were undone. If we did we got the whip again.

"The amount of beating we took! Not everybody could stick it out. But it made a diver out of me—and the best in the district. And earned me a pretty penny too."

Then the time had come when Baltasar had to give up the hazardous trade of a pearl-diver. He was no longer young and his left leg bore the terrible scars of a shark's teeth and his side the marks of an anchor chain. He bought a small shop in Buenos Aires and started a trade in pearls, corals, shells and sea curios. But shore life bored him and once in a way he decided he needed a break and put out to sea with pearl-divers.

He was always sure of a welcome, for what he didn't know about the Rio de la Plata and its pearling grounds was just not worth knowing. He was welcomed by all—he knew how to please divers and owners alike. The young divers he taught the tricks of the trade: how to hold their breath underwater and to fight off sharks, and—when in especially expansive mood—how to keep an extra fine pearl out of the boss's sight.

The owners he helped to sort out pearls and evaluate the best.

Baltasar was sitting on an upturned barrel, a thick cigar between his fingers, his face picked out of the darkness by the light of a lantern fixed to the mast. It was an elongated face with a finely cut nose and large handsome eyes—the face of an Araucanian. He was drowsing. But even when his eyes were asleep, his ears were not. They registered sounds and gave him warning in the deepest of sleep. There was nothing but the divers' sighing and murmuring to hear. The smell of rotting pearl oysters wafted from offshore. It was part of the job: the shell of a dead mollusc opens more easily. What would have been an overpowering stench for an unaccustomed nose was near perfume for Baltasar's. For him, a sea tramp that he was, it meant all the pleasures and dangers of life at sea.

After the last pearl was extracted the largest shells were brought on board the *Jellyfish*. Zurita wasn't one to let anything go to waste. He sold the shells to a factory where they made buttons and studs out of them.

Baltasar was asleep. The cigar had slipped from between his fingers. His chin rested on his chest.

A sound from far out at sea broke in on his sleep. Then it came nearer. Baltasar opened his eyes. What seemed to him the blast of a horn sounded again, followed by the cheerful ring of a young voice, repeated after an interval in a higher pitch.

The blast of the horn bore no resemblance to

11

the harsh blare of a ship's siren, nor the cheerful voice to the cries of a man, fallen overboard. In fact it didn't sound like anything Baltasar could think of. He rose. His sleep seemed blown away by a breeze. He went up to the rail and peered into darkness. His eye and ear detected nothing. Baltasar prodded with his foot a sleeping Indian into wakefulness.

"I heard a cry. That must be him," he told the diver softly.

"I can't hear a thing," the Gurona Indian, now up on his knees and listening, said as softly. Suddenly the horn and voice pierced the heavy silence again.

The Gurona shrank as from a whip lash.

"Yes, that's him," he said through his clattering teeth.

Other divers were waking up. They crawled towards the blotch of lantern light as though seeking in the yellowish beam protection from dreadful darkness. There they squatted, huddling together and straining their ears. The horn and voice came from far off again and was heard no more.

"That's him—the 'sea-devil'," the divers were whispering.

"We ought to be clearing out of here."

"A shark's a kitten compared to him!"

"Let's speak to the boss."

There was a patter of bare feet. Yawning and scratching a hairy chest Pedro Zurita came on deck. A pair of canvas trousers was all he had on; a revolver holster dangled from a broad leather belt. Zurita approached the divers. The lantern light revealed a swarthy face, crumpled with sleep, curls of thick hair escaping onto the forehead, black eyebrows, a pointed moustache and greying goatee.

"What's up?"

His self-assured voice and deliberate movements calmed the divers.

They spoke all at once.

Baltasar raised a hand to silence them.

"We've heard him—the 'sea-devil'," he said when order was temporarily restored.

"You dreamt it," Pedro said sleepily.

"We didn't. We all heard his horn," shouted the divers.

Again Baltasar waved them to silence.

"I heard the horn myself. That was him all right. There's nobody at sea can blow a horn like that. We ought to be getting away from here, and lose no time about it."

"Old wives' tales," said Pedro Zurita. He didn't like the idea of sailing from the pearling ground with all those oysters on board, stinking and still not ready for opening. But it was like running his head against a stone wall, trying to talk the divers into staying. They shouted discordantly, flung their arms about and threatened to abandon the schooner and walk to Buenos Aires if Zurita didn't weigh anchor.

"Curse you and the 'sea-devil'," he said finally. "You win. We'll weigh anchor at dawn." And grumbling and cursing he went below.

He was no longer sleepy. Lighting the lamp he got a cigar going and began pacing up and down his small cabin. His thoughts turned to the mysterious creature that had been haunting their part of the estuary for some time now, striking terror into the fishermen and seaside villagers.

Sailors and fishermen would tell tales about it, with many a timid glance over the shoulder, as if afraid that the monster might surprise them even as they spoke about it.

The creature was believed to have helped some people and harmed others.

"It's the sea-god," said the older Indians, "him as comes out of the ocean once in a thousand years—to restore justice on earth."

The Catholic priests exhorted their superstitious Spanish flock to seek salvation in religion, saying that the sea-monster was a visitation of the wrath of God for their neglect of the Holy Catholic Church.

Rumours spread and at last reached Buenos

Aires. For weeks the "sea-devil" made headlines in the sensation-hungry press. Any unaccounted-for loss of schooner or fishing-craft, any theft of nets or fish catch were all the "sea-devil's" doing. But there were other stories as well—of big fish mysteriously deposited in fishing boats, of men saved from drowning.

At least one of these swore that when he was going under for the last time somebody caught him from behind and sped him shorewards and onto the beach, disappearing behind the surf the very moment he struggled to his feet and looked back.

Nobody had seen the "sea-devil" or rather nobody was credited with having seen it. Though, of course, there were some who called heaven to witness that the creature had a head adorned with horns and a goat's beard, the legs of a lion and the tail of a fish or described it as an enormous toad with legs shaped like a man's.

At first the authorities paid no attention to all these rumours and newspaper articles, hoping for the sensation to fizzle out as newspaper sensations do. But rumours led to apprehension and apprehension to alarm, especially among the fishermen. They were afraid to put out to sea; catches declined; Buenos Aires was experiencing a shortage of fish. The authorities decided it was time to intervene. A force of coastguard cutters and police launches was mustered and given orders "to detain a person of unknown identity that is causing alarm and panic among the seaside population."

For a fortnight the task force combed the Rio de la Plata and the coast with nothing to their credit but several Indians detained for spreading rumours likely to cause alarm and panic.

The chief of the police issued an official announcement to the effect that the "devil" only existed in the rumours spread by some ignorant people, already detained and about to receive the punishment they deserved, and admonished the fishermen to scorn the rumours spread and resume their useful trade.

This helped for a time, but not for long: soon the "devil" was up to new pranks.

Some fishermen were wakened in the dead of night by the bleating of a kid that nothing short of magic could have put into their boat, lying as she was a goodish way offshore. Other fishermen hauled in their nets to find them slashed to pieces.

Overjoyed by the reappearance of the "devil" the newspapers now clamoured for the opinion of science. Nor had they to wait for long.

Scientists claimed that a sea-monster capable of intelligent acts could not exist in that part of the ocean unknown to science. They went on to say that this did not necessarily apply to greater ocean depths, though even there they would not expect to find such a monster. They tended to agree with the off-the-record opinion of the chief of the police who thought that some practical joker was at the bottom of it all.

But not all scientists shared that opinion. Some referred in their arguments to Konrad Hessner, world-famous naturalist, who left us descriptions of the sea-maiden, sea-devil, sea-monk and sea-bishop.

"When all is said and done many of the things propounded by ancient and medieval scientists have been borne out in our times for all modern science's endeavours to ridicule them out of existence. Divine creation is truly inexhaustible and we scientists, more than anybody else, are called upon to practise modesty and caution in our conclusions," they wrote.

These last apparently believed more in religion than in science and their lectures were more like homilies.

Finally a scientific expedition was equipped and dispatched to settle the scholarly wrangle.

The members of the expedition found no "devil" but they learned a great deal about the "unknown person's" doings (the older members insisted that the word "person" be changed for the word "creature").

17

The newspapers carried the expedition's report, which said:

"1. In several places on the beaches we examined we found narrow footprints of a distinct human shape. Though leading from and back to the sea, they might have been made by people from boats.

"2. The nets we examined had cuts of the type produced by sharp instruments. They might have been caught on sharp underwater crags or twisted metalwork of wrecks.

"3. A report—brought to our attention—of a dolphin that had been carried by a storm ashore, well clear of the water, and dragged back into the sea by someone who had left behind what looked like clawed footprints, has been carefully looked into.

"We are fully satisfied that the dolphin in question had been restored to its element by some kind-hearted fisherman. Nor would this have been the only instance of kindness on the part of fishermen towards dolphins. It is common knowledge that dolphins in pursuit of fish sometimes help the fishermen in that they drive fish to the shallows inshore. The alleged claws of the footprints could have been the work of the witnesses' imagination.

"4. The kid might have been brought by boat and slipped on board by some practical joker."

The scientists had a lot more to say in their attempts to explain away the "devil's doings." They were convinced that no sea creature could have performed them.

But the scientists' explanations did not satisfy everybody. They seemed insufficient even for some of the scientists. How could a practical joker—however resourceful and clever—keep dark his identity for so long? Yet what made the whole thing really baffling was that according to the expedition's findings—incidentally not included in their report—the "devil" sometimes performed several tricks of his at short intervals in places situated very widely apart. Either the "devil" could travel at an unheard-of speed or there were several of them at work. And that made the practical joker idea altogether too thick to believe.

That was what went through Zurita's mind as he paced up and down his cabin.

Dawn had come unnoticed and with it a pink beam of light, stealing through the port-hole. Pedro put out the lamp and started washing.

As he poured the tepid water over his head he heard cries of alarm coming from deck. Half-washed, he hurried up the companion ladder.

Pressing to the rail on the seaward side of the schooner the divers in loin-cloths were gesticulating amid a tumult of voices. Pedro looked down. There were no boats where they had been the previous night. Apparently they had gone adrift somehow in the night off-shore breeze. Now the morning breeze was slowly bringing them shorewards. Their oars were afloat, scattered all over the bay.

Zurita ordered the divers to collect the boats. Nobody budged. Zurita repeated his order.

"Why don't you go and try your own luck with the 'devil'?" somebody said.

Zurita placed a hand on his holster. The divers fell back against the mast, glowering at Zurita. A showdown seemed inevitable. Then Baltasar stepped into the breach.

"There isn't a thing will scare an Araucanian," he said. "A shark didn't fancy my old bones, neither will the 'sea-devil'." Lifting his arms he took a dive and swam towards the boats. The divers pressed to the rail again, watching Baltasar's progress with alarm. Handicapped though he was by age and an injured leg, he swam like a fish. A few powerful strokes brought the Indian alongside a boat. Picking up a floating oar he climbed into the boat.

"The painter's cut with a knife," he shouted. "Clean work—couldn't have been done better with a razor."

Seeing Baltasar safe and sound some of the divers followed suit.

Though only just risen the sun was scorchingly hot. There was not a cloud in the sky, not a ripple on the sea. The *Jellyfish* was a dozen miles or so south of Buenos Aires when, following Baltasar's advice, anchor was dropped in a small bay near a shore that rose in two rocky ledges straight from the water.

The boats scattered all over the bay. Each was manned by two divers, who did the diving and the hauling in turns.

The diver in the boat closest inshore seized a big piece of coral that was tied to the diving cord between his legs and made swiftly for the sea-bed.

The water was warm and so transparent that you could count the pebbles on the sea-bed. Closer inshore corals rose up like so many bushes of a petrified submarine garden. Small silver-bodied fish flashed in and out among the bushes.

The diver crouched on the sea-bed, quickly picking oysters and putting them into the small bag hooked to his leather belt. His tender, a Gurona Indian, his head and shoulders bent over the gunwale for a better view of the diver, held to his end of the diving cord.

Suddenly he saw the diver leap up, snatch at

the cord and give it a sharp tug that nearly pulled the Gurona overboard. The boat rocked. The Indian hurried hand over hand with the cord. Presently he was helping the heavily breathing man into the boat. His pupils were dilated, his dusky face ashen.

"Was it a shark?"

But the diver had not recovered sufficient wind to answer.

What could have scared him so badly? The Gurona bent low to the water surface for a better look. Something was definitely wrong down there. The small fry—like birds spotting a falcon—were speeding to the safety of submarine forest thickets.

Then he saw what looked like a cloud of purplish smoke billow into view from behind a submarine rock. As the cloud grew bigger the water turned a pinkish tint. Then a dark shape half-appeared from behind the rock, made a slow turn and slid back. That was a shark and the purplish cloud—blood spilt on the sea-bed. What could have happened down there? The Gurona looked at his mate. But he couldn't provide the answer. Lying on his back, he was snatching air with wide-open mouth, staring with unseeing eyes into the skies. There was nothing for it but to take him straight to the *Jellyfish.*

All the divers that were on board clustered round the man.

"Speak up, man," said a young Indian, shaking the diver. "Afraid your funky soul will part company with your body, if you open your mouth, eh?"

The diver shook his head, slowly recovering.

"I saw the 'sea-devil'," he said in a hollow faltering voice.

"The 'sea-devil'?"

"Come on then, for Christ's sake, tell us about him," the divers shouted impatiently.

"I looked up and saw a shark. Making straight for me. A big black brute with its huge jaws ready to snap. It sure seemed I'd had it. Then I saw him—"

"The 'devil'?"

"What does he look like? Has he got a head?"

"A head? Think he has. Eyes as big as saucers."

"If he has eyes he must have a head," was the young Indian's verdict. "Eyes don't come all by themselves. Any legs?"

"He's got front legs—like a frog's. Long green fingers, webbed and with claws. And he's all ablaze like a fish with scales. He makes for the shark, flashes with a front leg. Swish! There's a fountain of blood—"

"What do his hind legs look like?" a diver interrupted him.

"Hind legs?" He tried to remember. "There're no hind legs. Just a big tail—ending in two snakes."

"Who gave you the worst scare, him or the shark?"

"The monster!" came the unhesitating answer. "For all it saved my life."

"The 'sea-devil'," said an Indian.

"The sea-god that helps the poor," an old Indian corrected him.

By this time the news had reached the far-thest boats and more and more divers were coming on board, eager for the story.

The man was made to repeat his story over and over again. As he did so he recalled more details. It now appeared that the monster breathed fire and wriggled its ears, had sabre-like teeth, large fins and a tail like a rudder.

White-trousered and sombreroed Pedro Zurita shuffled back and forth in the background, his bare feet thrust into a pair of sandals, taking note of what was being said.

The more the diver recovered the use of his tongue the more Pedro became convinced that it was all a shark-scared diver's imagination. And yet it can't be only that, he thought. Somebody did slit that shark's side open—with all that pinkish water in the bay. The Indian's lying but there's obviously more to it than meets the eye. Rum business, dammit, he thought.

At that moment Zurita's train of thought was cut short by the blow of a horn coming from the direction of the reefs.

It had the effect of a thunderbolt. Tongues were paralyzed. Faces turned ashen-grey. Horror-stricken eyes stared in the direction of the reefs.

Near the reefs a family of dolphins were frisking in the water. One of the dolphins gave a loud snort as if in response to the horn summons, made for the reefs and was soon lost to sight behind them. After a few tense moments it reappeared. Riding it was the oddest creature, in fact, the very "sea-devil" just described by the diver. The monster had the body and head of a man, with a pair of immense eyes that blazed in the sun like a car's headlights; silvery-blue skin and dark-green forelegs, long-fingered and webbed. The creature's legs were immersed in the water, so there was no telling whether they were of man or of beast. In one of its forelegs the creature had a long winding shell. Giving another blow on it the creature laughed a gay manly laugh and suddenly shouted: "Full speed ahead, Leading!" in perfect Spanish, patted the dolphin's glossy back with its frog's hand and spurred its mount with its legs. And like a well-broken horse the dolphin put on speed.

A cry of surprise escaped the divers.

The creature looked round. The next they knew it was off the dolphin and on the other side of it. A green foreleg shot into sight to slap the dolphin's back. Obedient to it the, mount submerged.

The odd pair could just be seen making a quick half-circle and then it disappeared behind the reefs.

The whole thing had taken not more than a minute but the lookers-on stood rooted to the spot for some time.

Then hell broke loose. Some of the Indians shouted and ran about as though demented, others fell on their knees and prayed to God to spare their lives. A young Mexican, bawling with fright, took refuge high up the main mast. The Negroes crept below into the hold.

There could be no question of going on with the work. It was all Pedro and Baltasar could do to restore some order. The *Jellyfish* weighed anchor and sailed due north.

The master of the vessel went below, to his cabin, to think things over.

It's enough to drive one mad! he thought, pouring tepid water from a jug over his head. A sea-monster speaking the purest *Castellano*! What was it? The Devil's work? Hallucination? Can't happen to whole crews though. No two men even see the same dream. But we all saw the thing. That's a fact. So the "sea-devil" does exist after all, however impossible it may sound. Zurita poured more water over his head and leaned out of the port-hole for some fresh air. "Sea-devil" or not, he thought on, calming a bit, the monster appears to possess intelligence and an excellent command of Spanish. You should be able to talk to it. Suppose— Yes, why not? Suppose I catch it and make it dive for pearls. Why, a creature like that would be worth a whole shipful of divers. I'd be simply minting money! Every diver must have his fourth of the catch but this thing here'd only cost me its keep. That'd mean thousands, millions of *pesos* rolling in.

Zurita glowed with his vision of wealth. Not that it was the first time he had had it. Time and again he had dreamt of finding new, still untapped, pearling grounds. The Persian Gulf, the western coast of Ceylon, the Red Sea and the

27

coasts of Australia were far too distant for him
and pretty well fished clean at that. Even the
Gulf of Mexico, the Gulf of California and the
coast of Venezuela, where the best American
pearls were found, were too remote for his
ancient schooner. He'd need more divers too.
And Zurita had no money for that. So he kept in
home waters. But now it was different. Now
he could make his pile—once he had the "sea-
devil" in his hands.

He'd be the richest man in Argentina, perhaps in both Americas. Money would pave his
way to power. His name would sweep the
world. . . . But he had to play his hand careful
like—and first see to it that the crew didn't talk.

Zurita went on deck and had the whole crew
down to the cook called up.

"You all know," he told them, "what happened
to those who had been spreading rumours
about the 'sea-devil.' If you don't, they're still
in jail. Let me give you a word of warning. This
is it: anyone of you caught speaking of having
seen the 'sea-devil' will be clapped in jail to
feed vermin. Got that? So keep it under your
hats unless you want to get into trouble."

Nobody'd believe them anyway, not a fairy-
tale like that, Zurita thought, and, telling Baltasar to follow him, went below.

Baltasar listened to Zurita's plan in silence

"Sounds good," he said after a moment's thought. "The creature's worth a hundred divers. A 'devil' at your beck and call—not bad, eh? But you've got to catch it first."

"A sturdy net'll take care of that," said Zurita.

"He'll rip a net open as easily as he ripped that shark's belly."

"We can order a wire net."

"Who's going to do the catching? Not our divers. There's not one in the whole lot of 'em won't turn yellow at the mere name of it. They wouldn't dream of giving a hand, not for all the riches in the world."

"What about you, Baltasar?"

The Indian shrugged his shoulders.

"I've never hunted a 'sea-devil.' I expect it'll be no easy thing stalking him, seeing as you'll want him alive."

"You're not afraid, are you, Baltasar? What do you make of this 'sea-devil' anyway?"

"What can I make of a jaguar that takes to the air or a shark that climbs the trees? A beast you don't know is terrifying. But I like my game terrifying."

"I'll make it worth your while." Zurita placed an assuring hand on Baltasar's arm.

"The fewer people in on it, the better," he went on elaborating his plan. "You speak to the Araucanians we have on board. They've got more guts between them than the rest. Pick half a dozen from them, no more. If ours hold back, look about for others on shore. The 'devil' seems to be keeping close inshore. We'll try and locate his lair first. Then we'll know where to shoot our net." .

They wasted no time. Zurita had a wire bag net that looked like a big barrel with the bottom open made to order. Inside it he spread ordinary nets, in a way calculated to enmesh the devil. The divers were paid off. Baltasar had only managed to enlist two Araucanians from the crew. Another three he had signed on in Buenos Aires.

It was decided to start the devil hunt in the bay where they had first seen it. The schooner dropped anchor a few miles off the bay so as not to arouse the devil's suspicions. While Zurita's party occupied themselves with occasional fishing—to justify their hanging around—they took turns in watching the waters of the bay from the shelter of some rocks on the shore.

A second week was running out but there was still no sign of the devil.

Baltasar had struck up acquaintance with some Indians from a farming village nearby. He would sell them the daily catch at half-price and then stay behind for a chat, cleverly bringing up the subject of the "sea-devil." Soon the old Indian knew that they had been right in choosing the spot. Indeed, many villagers had heard the horn and seen the footprints on the beach. They said that the heels looked quite human but the toes were much too long. Sometimes they would find an imprint of the devil's back on the beach where he had lain.

The "devil" was not known to have done anybody any harm, so the villagers had long ceased to mind the traces he left behind. Besides, none of them had actually seen him.

For two weeks the *Jellyfish* had kept near the bay, going on with the make-believe fishing. For two weeks Zurita, Baltasar and the hired Indians had scanned the bay, but still no "seadevil" would show up. Zurita fretted and raged. He was as stingy as he was impatient. Every day cost money and that "devil" had kept them cooling their heels there many days now. Pedro was assailed by doubts. Suppose the creature was really a devil? Then no nets would catch him. Neither did superstitious Zurita particularly like the idea of meddling with one. Of course he could call a priest on board to bless the undertaking, but that would involve additional expense. And then, again, the creature might be some first-rate swimmer disguised as a "devil" to put fear into people for the sheer fun of it. There was the dolphin, of course. But that could have been tamed and trained like any other animal. Wouldn't it be better to drop the whole thing, he wondered.

Zurita promised a reward to the first man to spot the "devil" and, tormented with doubts, decided to wait a few days longer.

To his immense joy the third week brought signs of the "devil's" renewed activity.

One evening Baltasar tied up his boat, laden with that day's catch to be sold in the morning, and went to a nearby farm to visit an Indian friend. On his return he found the boat empty. Baltasar was convinced that it was the "devil's" handiwork though he couldn't stop marvelling at the amount of fish the "devil" had put away.

Later that evening the Indian on duty reported having heard the sound of a horn coming from the south. Two days later, early in the morning, the youngest Araucanian finally spotted the "devil." He came in from sea in the dolphin's company, not riding it this time but swimming alongside, grasping with one hand a broad leather collar round the dolphin's neck. In the bay the "devil" took the collar off the dolphin, patted it on the back, swam to the foot of a sheer cliff that jutted high on the shore and was seen no more.

On hearing the Indian's report Zurita promised not to forget about the reward and said:

"The 'devil' isn't likely to stir from his den to-day. That gives us a chance to have a look at the sea-bed. Now, then, who's willing?"

But that was a risk nobody was eager to take.

Then Baltasar stepped forward.

"I'm willing," was all he said. Baltasar wasn't one to go back on his word.

Leaving a watchman on board they went ashore and to the steep cliff.

Baltasar wound the end of a diving cord round his middle, took a knife, seized a stone between his knees and went down.

The Araucanians waited in tense silence for his appearance, peering into the water, murky blue where the cliff cast a deep shadow. A slow minute went by. At last there was a tug at the cord. When Baltasar had been helped ashore it was some time before he could say, panting:

"There's a narrow passage down there—leads into a cave—as dark as a shark's belly. And no other place for the 'devil' to be gone to—just a sheer wall of rock all round."

"Splendid!" exclaimed Zurita. "The darker, the better. We only have to cast the net and wait for the blighter to walk in."

Dusk was falling on the bay when the Indians lowered the wire net into the water across the mouth of the cave and secured the sturdy end ropes to rocks on shore. Then Baltasar tied a number of small bells to the ropes for early warning.

That done, Zurita, Baltasar and the five Araucanians settled down on the sand to await developments.

Nobody had been left on board the schooner this time. All hands were needed.

The night darkened swiftly. Presently the moon appeared and silvered the surface of the ocean. The hush of night enveloped the beach. The little party sat on in tense silence. Any minute now they might see that strange creature that had been striking terror into the fishermen and pearl-divers.

The night dragged on. People began drowsing.

All of a sudden the bells rang. The men sprang up, ran for the end ropes and heaved. The net felt heavy. The ropes tautened. Something seemed to be struggling in the net.

At last the net came up and the pale moonlight revealed in it the body of a half-man, half-beast writhing and struggling to get free. The enormous eyes and silvery scales glistened, moonlit. The "devil" made desperate attempts to free his right hand, caught in the wire meshes. Finally he succeeded, unsheathed the knife that hung on a narrow leather belt at his side and started hacking at the net.

"No, you don't, not a wire net," Baltasar muttered under his breath.

But to his surprise the "devil's" knife was whetted to the task. As the divers heaved at the net for all they were worth to get it on shore the "devil" was deftly widening the gash he had already made.

"Heave-ho, my hearties," Baltasar shouted urgently.

But at the very moment when their quarry seemed as good as in their hands the "devil" dropped through the gash into the water, sending up a cascade of sparkling spray, and was gone.

The men stopped heaving in desperation.

"That's some knife—cutting wire as you'd cut a loaf of fresh bread," Baltasar said admiringly. "The underwater blacksmiths must be a darned sight better'n ours."

Staring into the water Zurita had the air of a man who had lost all his fortune at one stroke.

Then he raised his head, tugged at his bristly moustache and stamped his foot.

"But no, damn you, this isn't the end!" he exclaimed. "I won't give up if I have to starve you in your bleeding cave. I'll spare no money,

I'll hire divers, I'll have nets and traps put everywhere but I'll get you!"

Whatever Zurita was lacking in, it was certainly not purpose and courage. This he had got with the hot blood of Spanish conquistadors that ran in his veins. And then he thought the thing was worth a fight, all the more so considering the "devil" was not half as formidable as he had feared.

A creature that could be made to tap the riches of the world for him would repay itself many times over. Zurita was going to have it, be it even guarded by Neptune himself.

DR. SALVATOR

Nor did Zurita go back on his word. He had had the mouth of the cave and the waters nearby crossed and recrossed with barbed wire and sturdy nets with ingenious traps guarding the few free passages left. But there was only fish to reward him for his pains. The "sea-devil" had not shown up once. In fact he seemed to have disappeared altogether. His dolphin friend put in a daily appearance in the bay, snorting and gambolling in the waters, apparently eager for an outing. But all in vain. Presently the dolphin would give a final snort and head for the open sea.

Then the weather changed for the worse. The easterner lashed up a big swell; sand whipped from the sea-bed made the water so opaque that nothing could be seen beneath the foamy crests.

Zurita could spend hours on the shore, watching one huge white-headed breaker after another pound the beach. Broken, they hissed their way through the sand, rolling over pebbles and oyster shells, onto his very feet.

"This can't go on," Zurita said to himself one day. "Something must be done about it. The creature's got his den at the bottom of the sea and he won't stir from it. Very well. So he who wants to catch him must pay him a visit. Plain as the nose on your face." And turning to Baltasar who was making another trap for the "devil" he said:

"Go straightway to Buenos Aires and get two diving outfits with oxygen sets. Ordinary ones won't do. The 'devil's' sure to cut the breathing tubes. Besides we might have to make quite a trip underwater. And mind you don't forget electric torches as well."

"Thinking of giving the 'devil' a look-up?" asked Baltasar.

"In your company, old cock. Yes."

Baltasar nodded and set off on his errand.

When he returned he showed Zurita besides

two diving suits and torches two long elaborately-curved bronze knives.

"They don't make their kind nowadays," he said. "These're ancient knives my forefathers used to slit open the bellies of your forefathers with–if you don't mind my saying so."

Zurita didn't care for the history part of it but he liked the knives.

Early at dawn the next day, despite a choppy sea, Zurita and Baltasar got into their diving suits and went down. It cost them considerable effort to find a way through their own nets to the mouth of the cave. Complete darkness met them. They unsheathed their knives and switched on their torches. Small fish darted away, scared by the sudden glare, then came back, swarming, mosquito-like, in the two bluish beams.

Zurita shooed them away: their silvery scales were fairly blinding him. The divers found themselves in a biggish cave, about twelve feet high and twenty feet wide. It was empty, except for the fish apparently sheltering there from the storm or bigger fish.

Treading cautiously they went deeper into the cave. It gradually narrowed. Suddenly Zurita stopped dead. The beam of his torch had picked out from the darkness a stout iron grille blocking their way.

Zurita could not believe his own eyes. He gripped at the iron bars in an attempt to pull the grille open. It didn't give. After a closer look Zurita realized that it was securely embedded in the hewn-stone walls of the cave and had a built-in lock.

They were faced with still another riddle.

The "sea-devil" had apparently even greater intelligence than they had ever credited him with. He knew how to forge an iron grille to bar the way to his underwater den. But that was utterly impossible! He couldn't have forged it actually under the water, could he! That meant he didn't live underwater at all or at least that he went ashore for long stretches of time.

Zurita felt his blood throb in his temples as though he had used up his store of oxygen in those few minutes under water.

He motioned to Baltasar and they went out of the cave, and came up.

The Araucanians who had been on tenterhooks waiting for them were very glad to see them back.

"What do you make of it, Baltasar?" said Zurita after he had taken off his helmet and recovered his breath.

The Araucanian shrugged his shoulders.

"We'll be ages waiting for him to come out, unless, of course, we dynamite the grille. We can't starve him out, all he needs is fish and there's plenty of that."

"Do you think, Baltasar, there might be another way out of the cave—inland I mean?"

Baltasar hadn't thought of that.

"It's an idea though. Why didn't we have a look round first," said Zurita.

So he started on a new search.

On shore Zurita came across a high solid white-stone wall and followed it round. It completely encircled a piece of land, no less than twenty-five acres. There was only one gate, made of solid steel plates. In one corner of it there was a small steel door with a spy-hole shut from inside.

A regular fortress, thought Zurita. Very fishy. The farmers round here don't normally build high walls. And not a chink anywhere to have a peep through.

There was not a sign of another habitation in the immediate neighbourhood, just bald grey rocks, with an occasional patch of thorny bush and cactus, all the way down to the bay.

Zurita's curiosity was roused. For two days he haunted the rocks round the wall, keeping a specially sharp eye on the steel gate. But nobody went in or out, nor did a single sound come from within.

One evening, on board the *Jellyfish*, Zurita sought out Baltasar.

"Any idea who lives in that fortress above the bay?" he asked.

"Salvator—so the Indian farm-labourers tell me."

"And who's he?"

"God."

The Spaniard's bushy black eyebrows invaded his forehead.

"Having your joke, eh?"

A faint smile touched the Indian's lips.

"I'm telling you what I've been told. Many Indians call Salvator a God and their saviour."

"What does he save them from?"

"Death. He's all-powerful, they say. He can work miracles. He holds life and death in the hollow of his hand, they say. He makes new, sound legs for the lame, keen eyes for the blind, he can even breathe life into the dead."

"*Carramba!*" muttered Zurita, as he flicked up smartly his bushy moustache. "There's a 'sea-devil' down the bay, and a 'god' up it. I wonder if they're partners."

"If you take my advice we'll clear out of here, and mighty quick, before our brains curdle with all these miracles."

"Have you seen anyone who was treated by Salvator?"

"I have. I was shown a man who had been carried to Salvator with a broken leg. He was running about like a mustang. Then I saw an Indian whom Salvator had brought back to life. The whole village say that he was stone-dead with a split skull. Salvator put him on his feet again. He came back, full of life and laughter. Got married to a nice girl too. And then all those children—"

"So Salvator does receive patients?"

"Indians. They flock to him from everywhere —from as far away as Tierra del Fuego and the Amazon."

Not satisfied with this information Zurita went up to Buenos Aires.

There too he learned that Salvator treated only Indians with whom he enjoyed the fame of a miracle-worker. Medical men told Zurita that Salvator was an exceptionally gifted surgeon, indeed a man of genius, but very eccentric, as is often the case with men of his calibre. His name was well known in medical circles on both sides of the Atlantic. In America he was famed for his bold imaginative surgery. When surgeons gave up a case as hopeless Salvator was asked to step in. He never refused. During the Great War he was on the French front where he operated almost exclusively on the brain. Thousands of men owed him their lives.

After the Armistice he went back home. His practice and real estate operations landed in his lap quite a fortune. He threw up his practice, bought some land near Buenos Aires, had a high wall built round it (another of his eccentricities), and settled down there. He was known to have taken up research. Now he only treated Indians, who called him God descended on earth.

Finally Zurita found out that before the War right where his present vast holding lay Salvator had had a house with an orchard also walled in on all sides. When Salvator had been away in France the house had been closely guarded by a Negro and a pack of ferocious bloodhounds.

Of late Salvator had lived a still more cloistered life. He wouldn't receive even his old university colleagues.

Having gleaned all this information, Zurita decided to fake illness so as to get inside the grounds.

Once again he was in front of the stout steel gate guarding Salvator's property. He rapped on the gate. Nobody answered. He kept rapping on it for some time and still there was not a stir inside. His blood up, Zurita picked up a stone and started battering the gate, raising a din fit to wake the dead.

Dogs barked somewhere well inside and at last the spy-hole was slid open.

"What do you want?" a voice asked in broken Spanish.

"A sick man to see the doctor—hurry up now, open the door."

"Sick men do not knock in this way," came the placid rejoinder and an eye peeped through at Zurita. "Doctor's not receiving."

"He can't refuse help to a sick man," insisted Zurita.

The spy-hole shut; the footsteps died away. Only the dogs kept up their furious barking.

Venting some of his anger in choice invective, the Spaniard set out for the schooner.

Should he lodge a complaint against Salvator in Buenos Aires, he asked himself once he was aboard. But what was the use? Zurita shook in futile rage. His bushy black moustache was in real danger now as he kept tugging at it in his agitation, making it fall like a barometer showing the doldrums.

Little by little, however, he quietened down and set to thinking what he should do next.

As he went on thinking his sunburnt fingers would travel up more and more often to give a flip to his drooping moustache. The barometer was rising.

At last he emerged on deck, and to every-body's surprise, ordered the crew to weigh anchor.

The *Jellyfish* stood for Buenos Aires.

"And about time too," Baltasar commented. "So much time and effort wasted. A curse on that 'devil' with a 'god' for a crony!"

THE SICK GRANDDAUGHTER

The sun was angrily hot. An old Indian, thin and ragged, was plodding along a dusty country road that ran through alternating fields of wheat, maize and oats. In his arms he carried a child covered against the sun with a little blanket very much the worse for wear. The child's eyes were half-closed; an enormous tumour bulged high on its neck. Whenever the old man stumbled the child groaned hoarsely and its eyelids quivered. Then the old man would stand still to blow into its face.

"If only I can get it there alive," he whispered and quickened his pace.

Once in front of the steel gate the old Indian shifted the child onto his left arm and gave the side door four raps with his right hand.

He had a glimpse of an eye through the spyhole, the bolts rattled and the door swung open.

The Indian stepped timidly inside. Standing

in front of him was a white-smocked old Negro
with a head of snow-white hair.

"I've brought a sick child," the Indian said.

The Negro nodded, shot the bolts home and
motioned to the Indian to follow.

The Indian looked round him. He found himself in a small prison-like court, paved with
big flagstones, with not a blade of grass anywhere. A wall lower than the outer one divided the court from the rest of the estate. At the
gateway in the inner wall stood a large-win-
dowed whitewashed building. Near it squatted
a group of Indians—men, women and children.

Some of the children were playing jack-
stones with shells, others were wrestling in silence. The old Negro saw to it that they did not
disturb the peace of the place.

The old man eased himself down submis-
sively in the shade of the building and started
blowing into the child's bluish inert face. An
old Indian woman squatting down beside him
threw a glance at the pair.

"Daughter?" she asked.

"Granddaughter," the Indian replied.

"It's the bog spirit as entered your child.
But he's stronger'n any evil spirit, he is. He'll
bring the poor thing back to health."

The Indian nodded.

The white-smocked Negro, who was making

a round of the sick, stopped in front of the Indian and beckoned to him to go in.

The room that the Indian entered was big and bare, except for a long narrow table, covered with a white sheet, standing in the centre of the flagged floor. A second, frost-glass panelled door was opened and in strode Dr. Salvator, a tall, broad-shouldered, dark-complexioned man wearing a white smock. The black eyelashes and eyebrows were the only hair on his head. He must have taken to shaving his head long ago, for it wore as good a coat of tan as his face. An aquiline nose, a jutting chin and tightly compressed lips lent to his face a cruel, one might say, predatory expression. The cold look of his brown eyes sent little shivers down the Indian's spine.

The Indian made a low bow and stretched his arms with the girl in them towards the doctor. With quick, sure and yet careful hands Salvator took the sick girl from the Indian's arms, unwound the rags with which she was swathed and tossed them very neatly into a receptacle in the corner. The Indian made to retrieve them but was stopped in his tracks by a peremptory "Leave them where they are."

Then Salvator laid the little girl on the table and bent over her. In profile now, he seemed to the Indian a bird of prey poised to strike.

Salvator was examining the tumour with his fingers. These too struck the Indian's imagination. They were long and amazingly supple and seemed to be able to bend not only downwards, but from side to side and even upwards. The Indian, normally a plucky man, tried to fight down the feeling of fear the extraordinary doctor had aroused in him.

"Excellent, splendid," Salvator was saying, as if in admiration of what he saw. The examination over, Salvator turned to the Indian.

"Come in a month's time, when the moon's new again, and you'll have your little girl back —healthy."

And he took the girl behind the frost-glass door.

Meanwhile the Negro had led in the next patient, the old woman with a swollen leg.

The Indian made a low bow in the direction of the frost-glass door and went out.

In exactly twenty-eight days the frost-glass door was opened again.

The little girl, sporting a new dress, lively and apple-cheeked, appeared in the doorway. There was alarm in her eyes as she caught sight of her granddad. The Indian lunged forward, picked the girl up, smacked her a kiss and examined her throat. The tumour was gone. There was only a tiny reddish scar where the girl had been operated upon.

The child kept pushing her granddad away with her hands and had even cried out when, kissing her, he pricked her with his stubbly chin. He had to let her down. Salvator came in. There was a flicker of a smile on his face as he patted the child's head and said:

"Here, take your child. You were only just in time bringing her. Another few hours and even I would not have been able to recall her to life."

The lips in the Indian's crinkled face quivered and tears came into his eyes. He gave the little girl another hug, then fell on his knees before Salvator.

"You saved my granddaughter's life," he said in a stifled voice. "A poor Indian has nothing but his own life to repay you with."

"What do I want with your life?" wondered Salvator.

"I may be old but there's strength in my arms yet," the Indian went on, not rising from his knees. "I'll take the little one to her mother— my daughter—and then come back. My life is now yours—for what you've done for me. I will serve you like a dog. Please don't say no, I beg you."

Salvator pondered.

He was chary of taking new servants. Not that he didn't need any. There was much work to do. Help Jim with the gardening, for instance. Come to think of it, he did need a servant. He would have preferred a Negro, to be sure, but this Indian fellow seemed all right. . . .

"You make me a gift of your life. Very well. I accept it. When can you come?"

"I'll be back before the first quarter's over," said the Indian, kissing the hem of Salvator's smock.

"What is your name?"

"Cristóbal, Cristo for short."

"Go, Cristo. I'll be waiting for you."

"Come on, my girlie," Cristo said to the child and picked her up again. She started to cry. Cristo hurried away.

AN ORCHARDFUL OF MIRACLES

When Cristo turned up again a week later Dr. Salvator greeted him with a searching glance and said:

"Now then, Cristo, pay attention to what I'm going to tell you. I'm taking you on. You'll have good pay and board—"

Cristo waved his hands.

"I don't want anything so long as you let me serve you."

"Be silent and listen," Salvator cut him short. "You'll have everything as I said you would. But there's one condition: keep your mouth shut about everything you see here."

"I'd sooner cut my tongue out with my own hands and throw it to the dogs than breathe a single word to anybody."

"See you don't have to do that," came Salvator's warning. With that he summoned in the white-smocked Negro and ordered him to take Cristo into the orchard and place him in Jim's charge.

Bowing silently, the Negro took the Indian outside and across the courtyard to the iron gate in the inner wall.

In response to the Negro's knock a barking of dogs came from behind the wall, then the gate creaked and opened slowly. The Negro gave Cristo a light push, shouted something in throaty tones to the Negro who stood inside the gate, and went away.

Cristo backed against the wall in fright. Charging at him were a pack of beasts with tawny black-spotted fur. Had they been in the pampas Cristo would not have hesitated in calling them jaguars. But these barked like dogs. Anyhow there was no time to puzzle it out. Cristo sprinted for the nearest tree and was up it with an agility surprising in a man of his age. The Negro hissed at them, for all the world like an angry cobra, at once bringing them to. The beasts stopped their thunderous baying, lay down and put their muzzles on their forepaws, slanting their eyes up at their master.

The Negro hissed again, this time to Cristo, and beckoned him to climb down.

"What're you hissing there like a snake for? Swallowed your tongue, eh?"

The Negro only gave an angry inarticulate sound.

He must be dumb, Cristo thought and remembered Salvator's warning. Does Salvator really cut out the tongues of those who betray his secrets? This poor blighter might be one of them. Sudden fear almost made Cristo lose his grip on the tree-trunk. He wished to God he were on the right side of the great wall again. With his eye he measured the distance between his tree and the wall but saw he couldn't make it. Meanwhile the Negro had approached the tree, got hold of Cristo's foot and was tugging at it impatiently. There was nothing for it but to take the hint. Cristo sprang down, grinned his most engaging smile, stretched out his hand and said amiably:

"Jim?"

The Negro gave a nod.

Cristo pumped his hand. Once in hell, play up to the devils, he thought. Aloud he asked:

"Dumb?"

There was no answer.

"Got no tongue?"

Still no answer.

Even if he's got no tongue, Gristo thought, he could at least talk in signs. Instead Jim took the Indian by hand, led him up to the tawny-skinned beasts and hissed something at them. The beasts rose, sniffed at Cristo and went calmly off. Cristo felt more at ease.

Then Jim led him on a round of the orchard.

After the bare stone-flagged yard the orchard looked a paradise of blossom and verdure. Stretching eastwards, it gently sloped down almost to the very shoreline. Narrow alleys strewn with finely crushed reddish shells and lined with weird cacti, fleshy bluish-green agaves and yellowish-green flowers criss-crossed it between groves of peach and olive trees. These gave shade to lush grass—its deep green broken here and there by little white-stone ponds—and beds of bright many-coloured flowers. A few fountains were sending high their jets of sparkling water to lend freshness to the air.

The orchard vibrated with the singing of birds and the roaring of beasts.

Never in his life had Cristo seen the strange birds and animals that met his eye at every turn.

A six-legged lizard scuttled across the path, its greenish skin coppery in the bright sun. A double-headed snake was hanging from a tree, making Cristo jump as it hissed at him with its two throats. A still louder hiss from the Negro, however, silenced it; dropping from the tree it disappeared among a border of rushes. Another long snake hurried away from the path where it had been basking, helping itself along with a pair of legs. In a little enclosure, near the walk, a pig was grunting, its large single eye fixed at Cristo.

Then a pair of large white rats, joined side to side, scuttered towards them along the reddish walk, looking for all the world like a double-headed, eight-legged monster. From time to time this dual creature went through a struggle; each rat tried to pull its way, both squeaking their displeasure. But the right side invariably won. Grazing near the path was another pair of Siamese twins, fine-fleece sheep this time. Unlike the rats they never quarrelled; they must have reached a common mind long, long ago. But it was the monster they met next that struck Cristo's imagination most. It was a big pink dog with not a single hair on it but what looked like a little monkey—or the upper part of one at any rate—sticking out from its back. The dog came up to Cristo and wagged its tail, while the little monkey kept jerking its head right and left, waving its arms, patting the dog on the back and jibbering at Cristo. The Indian dug a hand into his trouser pocket, brought out a piece of sugar and was offering it to the monkey when somebody stopped his hand and hissed. It was Jim, whom Cristo, engrossed by all those queer creatures, had clean forgotten. The old Negro explained by signs that he was not to feed the monkey. Cashing in on the interlude a parakeet-headed sparrow swooped down at the piece of sugar which Cristo still had between his fingers and carried it off to safety behind a bush. From farther away, in the middle of a meadow, came the lowing of a horse with a cow's head.

A pair of llamas swept across the meadow, their horse's tails spreading out in flight. Strange creatures were crowding on Cristo from all sides: dogs with cat's heads, cocks waddling on webbed feet, horned boars, eagle-beaked ostriches, puma-bodied sheep.

Cristo thought he was having a nightmare; he rubbed his eyes, sprinkled his head with cool water from a pond but nothing helped. In the ponds he saw snakes with fishes' heads and gills, fish with frogs' legs, enormous toads with bodies as long as a lizard's.

And Cristo again wished himself well outside the walls.

Finally, Jim brought the Indian to a broad sand-strewn stretch in the middle of which stood a white-marble Moorish-style villa, its arches and colonnades half-screened behind the trunks of palm trees. Brass dolphin-shaped fountain spouts sent cascades of water into the pools where goldfishes frisked in the pellucid water. The biggest fountain of them all, opposite the main entrance, had the shape of a youth astride a dolphin—perhaps it was Triton, the marine god of the ancients—with a winding horn pressed to his mouth. Obviously the work of a master sculptor, the group looked all but alive.

Behind the villa there were a few outhouses and still farther, a jungle of thorny cacti, with a white wall at the far end, showing through at places.

Another wall, thought Cristo.

Jim led him into a small cool room. In his sign language he explained that Cristo was to live there and then left him alone.

By and by Cristo began finding his way about in the new strange world. It didn't take him long to find out that the animal population of the orchard was quite tame. With some he was soon even on terms of friendship. The dogs with jaguar skins, the cause of such scare on his first day in the orchard, followed him about, licking his hands. The llamas ate out of his hand. The parrots perched on his shoulder.

The orchard and the animals were tended by twelve Negroes as dumb as Jim. At any rate Cristo never heard them speak. They all went silent about their business. Jim was a sort of superintendent over them. He gave them their work and saw that they did it. Cristo, much to his own surprise, had been appointed his deputy. His duties were not hard. There wasn't too much work and the food was plentiful. But the oppressive silence of the Negroes soon began to get him down. Besides, he was convinced that they had all had their tongues cut out. And every time Salvator summoned him to the office—not that it was often—Cristo thought his turn had come. But then something happened to allay his fears.

One day he came across Jim lying fast asleep in the shade of an olive tree. The Negro was lying on his back, his mouth hanging open. Cristo used the opportunity of looking for the Negro's tongue and, to his relief, found it there all right.

Dr. Salvator's day was well-planned and busy. From seven to nine he received patients, from nine to eleven he operated upon those who required it. Then he went to his villa to do laboratory work. This involved operating on animals and studying them. An experiment over, the animals went back to the orchard. Cristo, who dusted the rooms in the villa, managed occasionally to slip into the laboratories. The things he saw there would haunt his imagination for long afterwards. Hearts and kidneys carved out of their bodies lived on in glass jars. Amputated limbs seemed to be waiting for their owner.

His skin crawling Cristo hurried out. He preferred to be among the live monsters of the orchard.

Salvator seemed to trust the old Indian, but not beyond the third wall. And it was just what was on the other side that Cristo was so eager to see. One midday, when everybody was having a siesta, he stole up to the wall. Children's voices floated over to him. They spoke an Indian dialect he knew but intermingling with them, as if in a quarrel, there were other voices, thin and squeaky, speaking what seemed to Cristo a very peculiar brand of Indian.

Coming across Cristo in the orchard one day Salvator halted and, looking him straight in the eye as was his wont, he said:

"You've been with me a month now, Cristo, and I'm pleased with your work. One of the servants in the lower orchard has fallen ill. You will replace him. You will see many new things there. But mind that little conversation we had about your tongue unless you want to lose it."

"I've almost forgotten the use of it with all your dumb Negroes around, Doctor," said Cristo.

"Excellent. Silence pays, you know. Incidentally, do you know your way in the Andes?"

"I was born and bred in the mountains."

"Splendid. I will soon want to replenish my zoo with a new batch of birds and animals. I'm going to take you with me. You may go now. Jim will take you to the lower orchard."

Accustomed though he was to the wonders of the place, Cristo had more surprises coming.

In the spacious sunlit meadow naked children were playing with monkeys. Almost all Argentina's Indian tribes seemed to be represented there by children ranging in age from about three to twelve years. All of them were patients of Salvator's. Many had undergone complicated operations and owed their very lives to Salvator's skill. Once round the corner the children recuperated playing in the orchard till they were strong enough to be taken home.

Tailless monkeys with not a tuft of hair on their bodies kept them company. But what really amazed Cristo was that all of them could speak some kind of Indian. They joined in the children's games, quarrelling with them and shouting in thin high-pitched voices, though on the whole they were quite a friendly crowd.

Sometimes Cristo was inclined to think they were human beings after all.

The lower orchard, as Cristo soon found out, was smaller than the other one, sloped steeper seawards and ended in a big cliff rising sheer like a wall. Somewhere behind it was the invisible ocean, revealed by the roar of the surf.

A closer look showed that the cliff was manmade and, in fact, nothing more than another wall, a fourth one, for in it Cristo found an iron door, painted grey to blend with the cliff and furthermore screened by a thick growth of wistaria.

Cristo listened. The roar of the surf was the only sound. Where did the small door lead to? The seaside?

Suddenly there was a hubbub of children's voices behind him. Cristo wheeled round and saw the children staring up into the sky. He also looked up and spotted a small red balloon slowly floating up and across the orchard. The wind was heading it seawards.

An ordinary children's balloon, it seemed to stir Cristo deeply. As soon as the servant that had been ill reported to work, the old Indian went to see Salvator.

"Soon we're leaving for the Andes, Doctor. It might be some time before we come back. May I go and see my daughter and her child?"

Salvator didn't like his servants leaving the premises, and he didn't speak at once. Cristo stood waiting, his eyes boldly meeting the cold stare of Salvator's.

"Remember your pledge," said Salvator. "I wouldn't like you to lose your tongue. You may go, but see you're back within three days. Wait!"

Salvator went into the other room and brought back with him a suède leather pouch.

"There's something for your granddaughter— and for your silence too."

AN AMBUSH

"If he doesn't come this time I'll cut the painter as far as the pair of you are concerned, I'll be damned if I won't. I'll get smarter people onto the job," Zurita was saying, tugging impatiently at his bristly moustache. He wore a white town suit and a panama hat. They had met well outside Buenos Aires, at a point where the pampas were taking over from the maize fields.

Baltasar, in a white blouse and a pair of blue-striped trousers, was squatting by the roadside, plucking dejectedly at the sun-parched brittle blades of grass.

He himself was beginning to regret having sent his brother to spy on Salvator.

Though Baltasar's elder by ten years, Cristo was strong and lithe and as cunning as a pampas-cat. But he was not reliable. He couldn't settle down to anything. There had been a time he took up farming but soon dropped it, thoroughly bored. Then he ran a dockside tavern till he drank himself out of house and home. Lately Cristo had been earning a precarious living on the windy side of the law. With his sharp wits he could ferret out anything but was not to be trusted with much. He might even betray his own brother if it were made worth his while. Baltasar knew his man and was as worried as Zurita.

"Are you sure Cristo saw that balloon, anyhow?"

Baltasar shrugged his shoulders. He would have much preferred to drop the whole affair there and then, go home and have a glass of cold water laced with wine in the peace and quiet of his shop.

A cloud of dust mushroomed over the turn of the road and was lit up by the last rays of the setting sun. A shrill drawn-out whistle was heard.

Baltasar livened up.

"That's him!" he said.

"Not too damned soon either," said Zurita.

Striding briskly towards them was Cristo— no longer a doddering old Indian with a sick grandchild come to see the doctor. Giving another whistle Cristo came nearer and saluted the pair.

"Well, have you seen the 'sea-devil'?" Zurita asked him by way of greeting.

"Not yet, but he's there all right. Salvator keeps him behind four walls. The main thing is Salvator trusts me. That sick granddaughter did it." Cristo laughed, narrowing his sly eyes. "She nearly gave the whole show away though. When she recovered, I mean. Here's me, picking her up and kissing her like a loving granddad and she kicks away and fairly bursts into tears," and he laughed again.

"Where did you get the girl?" asked Zurita.

"Money's hard to get, girls aren't," said Cristo.

"And her mother's happy too. I got five *pesos*—she got her daughter back healthy."

That he had also received a sizeable sum from Salvator he didn't trouble to mention. All the more understandable this, since he wasn't going to share it with the child's mother.

"A regular zoo that place—chock-full of monsters." And Cristo started his story.

"That might all be very interesting," Zurita said after some time and lighted a cigar, "but you haven't seen the goods. What do you propose to do next?"

"Make a trip to the Andes." And Cristo told them of Salvator's plan.

"Splendid!" exulted Zurita. "We'll attack the place as soon as Salvator's party leaves and carry the 'sea-devil' away by force. The place's so out-of-the-way one could do it in broad daylight and nobody the wiser."

Cristo shook his head.

"The jaguars will bite your heads off. Even if they don't you won't find the 'sea-devil'—not until I've found out where he is."

"Then here's what we'll do," Zurita said, after thinking it over for a while. "We'll ambush Salvator's party, take him prisoner and hold him to ransom. The 'sea-devil' 'll be the price."

With a slick movement of his hand Cristo drew a cigar out of Zurita's breast pocket.

"Many thanks. An ambush's better. But Salvator's sure to pull some trick on you—promise to deliver the goods and never do it or something. Those Spaniards—" the rest of the sentence was lost in coughing.

"Well, what do *you* suggest?" Zurita said irritably.

"Patience. Salvator trusts me but only as far as three walls go. He must be made to trust me as he trusts his own shadow, then he'll show me the 'sea-devil' of his own free will."

"Well?"

"Well, Salvator will be attacked by bandits," he jabbed his finger at Zurita's chest, "and delivered from them by an honest Araucanian"— he tapped his own chest. "Then there will be no secrets for Cristo in Salvator's house. And no lack of golden *pesos*," he added in an aside for himself.

"That's not a bad idea."

Then they agreed on the road Cristo should suggest to Salvator.

"On the eve of the departure I'll throw a red stone over the wall. Have everything ready." And Cristo was gone.

Though the plan of attack was well worked out an unforeseen circumstance nearly made it fall through.

Zurita, Baltasar and a dozen cutthroats

hired in the dockside, wearing Gaucho clothes all well armed and mounted, had taken up stations alongside the pampas road. The night was dark. The gang listened hard for the hoofbeats.

Suddenly the bandits heard the chugging of an engine, quickly drawing nearer. Two powerful headlights stabbed the darkness and before they knew where they were a big black car had rushed by.

It had never entered Cristo's head that Salvator could travel in this new, unconventional way.

Zurita was beside himself with rage and disappointment; Baltasar was amused.

"Take it easy, master," he said. "They travel by night and will rest in the day-time. We'll overtake them." And he spurred his horse on; the rest followed suit.

They had ridden hard for the better part of two hours when they spotted the glow of a campfire ahead.

"That's them. Something's happened. Wait for me here while I do some scouting."

And dismounting, Baltasar crawled snake-like into the darkness.

He returned in an hour.

"The car's out of order. They're repairing it. Cristo keeps watch. Come on, let's hurry and get it done with."

It was a quick job. The bandits took Salvator's party by surprise—just when they had repaired the car—and tied Salvator, Cristo and the three Negroes hand and foot with not a shot fired.

One of the bandits, who acted chieftain, Zurita preferring to stay in the background, told Salvator that they were prepared to ransom him for a big sum of money and named it.

"You'll have it," said Salvator.

"That's for you. And it's double if you want your men set free too," said the bandit following up his advantage.

"I haven't got that much money available," Salvator said, after a pause.

"Finish him off!" the bandits shouted all at once.

"I'll give you till dawn to think it over," said the bandits' spokesman.

Salvator shrugged his shoulders as he repeated:

"I haven't got that much available."

His coolness impressed even the bandits.

Taking Salvator and his men aside, the bandits ransacked the car and found the spirits intended for collections. Soon they were drunk and sleeping on the ground.

At crack of dawn somebody crawled softly to Salvator's side.

"It's me," came Cristo's voice. "I managed to untie myself and have killed the bandit on watch. The rest are drunk and incapable. Let's hurry!"

They got in, the Negro driver started the engine, the car leapt forward.

Behind there were shouts and a few rifle shots rang out.

Salvator pressed Cristo's hand.

Only after Salvator's departure did Zurita learn that Salvator had been willing to pay. Wouldn't it have been simpler just to take it than try to kidnap a "sea-devil" nobody knew was worth anything? It's all over bar the shouting, though, he thought. And he waited for news from Cristo.

THE AMPHIBIAN

Cristo had hoped that Salvator would send for him and say:

"You've saved my life, Cristo. From now on there will be no secrets for you in this place. Come with me, I'll show you the 'sea-devil'." Or words to that effect.

But Salvator fell short of Cristo's hopes. He generously rewarded the brave Araucanian and became all wrapped up in his research again.

So Cristo started his own research. The secret door proved a hard nut to crack but his patience was rewarded in the end. One day he pressed a boss on it and it swung slowly open, like the door to a strong room. Cristo slipped through and the door swung shut, taking him a little aback. He examined it, pressing every boss in turn; the door didn't open.

"A fine trap I caught myself in," he muttered. "Well, I might as well have a look round."

He found himself in a hollow, thickly overgrown with trees and bushes and walled in on all sides with man-made cliffs.

The plants Cristo saw were of the kind usually growing on humid soils. The big shady trees did not let sunlight through to the numerous rivulets burbling underneath. Fountains, scattered among the trees, added to the moisture in the air. The place was as damp as the low banks of the Mississippi. Standing in the middle of the grounds was a small flat-roofed stone house with lichen-clad walls. The green blinds on the windows were pulled down. The house had a not-lived-in look.

Cristo reached the far end of the orchard. Judging by the rustle of pebbles that came to him from behind the wall the ocean was close at hand. So this is as far as Salvator's holding goes, thought Cristo. In front of the wall was a huge square tree-lined swimming pool no less than fifteen feet deep.

At Cristo's approach some creature he didn't have time to see beyond a glimpse dashed from under the trees and across to the swimming pool, making a big splash as it plunged in. Cristo's heart was beating nineteen to the dozen as he went closer. That must be him, the "sea-devil," he thought. He was going to see him at last.

The Indian looked into the clear water.

On the bottom on white stone tiles crouched a big monkey. There was fear mingled with curiosity in its return glance. And it was breathing—breathing under the water! Spell-bound, Cristo couldn't tear his glance away from its sides, heaving and falling, heaving and falling. . . .

Presently, with a start, Cristo recovered himself and gave a short laugh. So the "sea-devil," that fisherman's bogey, was just a monkey that could breathe underwater.

Cristo was at once glad and disappointed. Descriptions of the monster had led him to expect something quite different. What tricks fear and fancy play on us, thought the old Indian.

Now it was time for him to make good his retreat. Cristo retraced his steps to the secret door, climbed a big tree by the wall, got onto it and jumped down, hoping to God his old legs would not trip on him.

No sooner Cristo was safely on the ground than he heard Salvator's voice.

"Hey, Cristo, where are you?"

The Indian grabbed a rake lying on the path and applied himself to gathering dry leaves.

"I'm here," he shouted.

"Come along, Cristo," Salvator said, striding onto the path and across to the secret door. "To open you press here," and he pressed the very boss Cristo had just used.

A bit late, aren't you, I've seen your devil, thought Cristo.

They went into the orchard. Salvator led the way past the lichen-clad house straight to the swimming pool. The monkey was still underwater, crouching where he had left it, letting out little bubbles of air at each exhalation.

At the sight of the monkey Cristo went through a little show of surprise, which, almost at once, turned to genuine.

For Salvator was paying no attention to the monkey, apart from waving his hand at it as if dismissing it. Promptly the monkey swam up, scrambled out, shook itself and climbed a tree. Salvator bent down and pressed in a small green panel, concealed in the grass. There was a hollow rumble and hidden hatches yawned open all along the bottom of the pool. The water gushed through. In a few minutes the pool was dry. The hatches snapped shut. An iron ladder, reaching down to the bottom, slid into view from its place somewhere in the side of the pool.

"Come on, Cristo."

They climbed down. Salvator stepped on a tile and another hatch opened—in the centre of the pool. Iron steps led down into the darkness.

Cristo followed Salvator down into a corridor, faintly illumined by the light falling through the hatch. As they proceeded it soon gave way to complete darkness. The echo of their footsteps rang dully in the corridor.

"We're nearly there, Cristo."

Salvator halted and ran his hand along the wall. There was a click and floods of brilliant light. They stood in a stalactite cave, facing a brass door with lions' heads gripping brass rings in their jaws. Salvator pulled at one of the rings. The stout door swung open, letting them into a dark hall. There was another click as a globular opaque lamp lit up a big cave whose far wall was all glass. Salvator worked the switches. The cave was dark again, then several powerful searchlights threw their beams into what looked an immense aquarium just behind the glass wall. Fish frisked among the seaweeds and corals. Suddenly Cristo saw a human-like creature, with huge globular eyes and frog's paws, step out from behind a tangled growth of seaweeds. The creature swam with easy grace towards the glass wall, in a close-up of immense eyes and silvery-blue scales, nodded to Salvator, entered an all-glass cubicle that was at one side of the wall and shut the glass door. The cubicle was quickly emptying. The stranger opened the other door and was in the cave.

"Take off your gloves and goggles," said Salvator.

The newcomer obediently took the things off and Cristo faced a slim good-looking young man.

"Please meet Ichthyander the amphibian, or the 'sea-devil' as he is also known," Salvator introduced the young man to Cristo.

The young man was smiling amiably as he offered his hand to the Indian.

"Hullo," he said in Spanish.

Cristo pressed the offered hand. He was too stunned for speech.

"The Negro who's serving Ichthyander is ill," went on Salvator. "You'll stay with

Ichthyander for a time. I'll make it permanent
if you give satisfaction."

Cristo nodded in silence.

A DAY OF ICHTHYANDER'S

It is still night but dawn is near.

The air, warm and damp, is full of aromas
of magnolia, tuberose and mignonette. Not a
leaf stirs. All is quiet; the crunch of sand un-
derfoot is the only sound. Swinging from his
belt in time to his step as he goes along the
garden walk are his dagger, a pair of goggles
and webbed gloves and swimming shoes. The
path runs between black blobby shapes of
trees and bushes, only visible by comparison.
Ichthyander brushes a branch every now and
then, sprinkling dewy drops on his hair and
cheek, still warm with sleep.

The path veers to the right and dips a little.
The air gets perceptibly damper. Ichthyander
feels stone flags and halts. Unhurriedly he
dons his swimming gear. Then he exhales all
the air from his lungs and plunges into the
pool. The water is invigoratingly cool, sending a prickly sensation through his gills,
which are now moving rhythmically. Man has
turned fish.

A few powerful strokes take Ichthyander

down to the very bottom of the pool and a little way along it. His outstretched hand meets the first iron bracket sunk in the stone wall, then another, then a few more, till he's in the tunnel and walking bent forward against the incoming cold current. A push with both feet and he's up but feeling as if he has plunged into a warm bath. It's where the warmer water from the ponds travels to the open sea. Ichthyander turns over on his back, folds his arms and drifts head first, letting the warm current do his work for him.

The end of the tunnel is drawing near. He can already hear the rustle of stones and shells where the spring in the sea-floor at the tunnel-mouth throws up its jet of hot water.

The amphibian turns over for a better view. But it's still pitch dark. He stretches his arm forward and the next moment finds the iron grille, its bars thick with slimy seaweeds and rough barnacles. For some time he fumbles with the intricate lock. Presently the heavy circular door swings slowly open, Ichthyander slips through and as he heads for the ocean hears the lock click behind him.

It is still dark underwater. Only below, in the black depths, there is an occasional bluish sparkle of *Noctilucae* and the dull reddish glow of a passing jellyfish. But dawn is almost there and the phosphorescent creatures of the sea one by one extinguish their tiny lamps.

Breathing comes less easy to Ichthyander; there are constant little pricks in his gills. That means he's already past the rocky headland and in the stream of muddy water from a river that flows into the ocean there.

I wonder how the river fish can live in that silty water at all, he thinks. Must have tougher gills.

Ichthyander turns sharply to his right, due south, then goes down till he strikes the clean water cold current that travels along-shore northwards to a point where it veers to the east under the impact of the mighty Paraná River pouring into the ocean. Its bottom layer flows rather deeply, but its top layer—Ichthyander's destination—is only about fifty feet below the surface. He can rest now: the clear waters of the current will take him a long way out into the ocean.

He can even have a nap while it's still dark and the fish of prey are not up and about yet. Sleep comes sweetest when dawn is near.

While he sleeps his skin registers every little change in temperature and water pressure. Presently his ears detect a hollow clank, then

another and still another. Those are anchor-
chains. A few miles away, in the bay where
he's drifting to, asleep, smacks are weighing
anchor for dawn fishing. Then, superimposing
on all other sounds, comes a steady rumble,
far-off but powerful. That comes from the
screws of the *Horrocks*, a large British liner
plying between Liverpool and Buenos Aires.
The liner must still be another twenty miles
off but that's nothing for sound: in sea-water
it travels at a speed of some fifty miles per
minute. By night the *Horrocks* is a sight to
feast your eyes on—a gay town, brightly illu-
minated and floating. But to see her at night
Ichthyander has to leave for the ocean in the
evening. It is a different *Horrocks* that makes
harbour in Buenos Aires soon after sun-up—all
her lights out, bulky and blaring. But he'd
better come out of his nap. The liner will soon
have all the inhabitants of the ocean wide
awake, what with her screws, engines and
lights. Surely the slight change of pressure
that alerted him a few moments ago was caused
by dolphins, always the first to sense the
approach of the liner. They must be well on
their way to the liner by now, eager to meet
her.

*　*　*

As the harbour and bay come to life the chugging of ships' engines closes upon Ichthyander. He opens his eyes, shakes his head to drive away the last of sleep and propells himself up.

Surfacing, he takes a careful look round for any boat or schooner, sees none anywhere near enough to bother, and treads water.

There are only cormorants and sea-gulls round him, skimming the water often so closely that their chests or wing-tips touch its mirror-like surface, sending tiny wavelets scurrying away. The cawing of the white sea-gulls is like a child crying. Swishing with its mighty wings through the air directly above Ichthyander so that he fancies he's struck by a minor gale, a huge snow-white albatross heads shorewards. The red-beaked orange-clawed bird has black-fringed wings, every inch of twelve feet from tip to tip. It's not without envy that Ichthyander watches it go. What wouldn't he give to have just such wings!

Night is retreating behind the distant mountains in the west. The eastern sky is slowly turning rosy. Barely perceptible ripples appear on the ocean, like so many tiny streaks of gold. When the sea-gulls soar up they turn pink.

Blue patterns crease the pale level surface of the sea as a gentle breeze starts to blow. It gathers force; the restless blue becomes deeper. The first yellowish tongues of foam begin to lap the beaches. The water closest inshore turns green.

A string of schooners comes in sight, low on the water. Ichthyander remembers his father's orders to avoid people and goes down in a steep dive. Soon he's back in the cold current that will carry him further offshore, eastwards. In the lilac twilight that reigns at this depth red, yellow and brown fish flitter about like a motley swarm of butterflies.

A buzzing sound comes from above; for a moment the water darkens. That must be a sea-plane flying low.

Once, he recalls, a sea-plane landed on the water close to him. He went for a closer look, held onto a float—and came very near to losing his life. All of a sudden the sea-plane took off and Ichthyander was whisked some thirty feet aloft before he recovered enough presence of mind to jump for his life.

* * *

Ichthyander looks up. The diffused ball of sun is almost plumb overhead, indicating that midday is close at hand. The surface of the water is no longer a vast mirror that faithfully reflects the sea-bed where it is raised, the bigger fish and Ichthyander. Like a funhouse mirror it is now distorted and assuming an infinite variety of shapes.

Ichthyander comes up. As he draws near the surface he becomes aware of a choppy sea. Presently his head and shoulders are clear and he's riding up on the crest of a wave, then down, then up again. . . . Oho, the sea *is* choppy! There's quite a surf already where the swell of the sea breaks upon the shore, roaring lustily, overturning big boulders. The water next to the white foamy line has been churned a yellowish green while a sharp south-westerner goes on whipping up waves, tearing off white tips of foam. Every now and then spray blows into Ichthyander's face, giving him intense pleasure.

Why is it, Ichthyander wonders, that when you swim through the waves they seem deep-blue but when you look back they are much paler?

Shoals of flying fish skim away. Gliding up over the wavetops and down across the troughs they fly some forty feet and touch down, and fly up again. The gulls dart about, crying. The fastest birds there are—frigates—cut the air with their wide wings. The one over there—with a huge curved beak and sharp claws, dark-brown feathers shot with green and an orange-hued crop—is a male. His mate, white breasted and with paler plumage, keeps at his side. Suddenly she drops down like a stone and the next moment is up again, a silver-scaled fish struggling in her beak. Albatrosses are soaring aloft, a sure sign of a storm brewing.

Somewhere up there, dauntless birds with the undignified name of screamer are already speeding to meet the inky clouds. The fishing smacks are less eager to encounter the storm. Under a full press of sail they seek the shelter of the harbour.

Greenish twilight reigns below the waves and the amphibian tells his way by the big ball of sun that can still be seen through the double screen of gathering cloud and water. He's got to reach the oyster-ground before the sun is blotted out by clouds if he's to have his lunch at all. Swimming frog-wise he spurts on.

From time to time he turns over on his back to take his bearings by the blob of sunlight overhead which is only a shade lighter than the surrounding bluish-green semi-darkness. His gills and skin are of great help too, registering little changes in water content.

Near oyster-grounds water is richer in oxygen and feels altogether lighter and more pleasant to the body, but there's more salt in it. So Ichthyander tastes the water. Like an old sea-wolf that can tell the approach of land by signs revealed only to him, Ichthyander is sure of his way.

At last to his right and left loom up the long-familiar outlines of underwater cliffs. There is a piece of level ground between them with another wall of a cliff behind. Ichthyander calls the spot his underwater harbour, for it's calm in the worst of storms.

It's a harbour for multitudes of fish as well, the water is as thick with them as a kettle of chowder! Small ones, with a yellow band across the body and a yellow tail; others with several dark bands running almost diagonally, and numerous brighter kinds, magenta, orange, azure. They shy away in shoals, then reappear from nowhere again. When you come up, fish are milling round you all the way, but you look down and there are none. Ichthyander puzzled over this for a long time till he caught a fish. Its body was the size of his palm but flat as a pancake. Then he knew.

Now for his lunch. On the patch of level sea-floor oysters are plentiful. Ichthyander settles down beside a thriving colony, reclines at ease and prises open the first mollusc that comes to his hand. The choice titbit goes into his mouth. He has a way of eating underwater that makes it an easy thing. Taking a mouthful he ejects water through half-clenched teeth with a movement that has become automatic with him. Naturally he swallows a little water with his food but he's used to it.

Seaweeds sway round him, the perforated greenery of the Agars, the pinnate grass-green leaves of the Mexican Caulerpa and a tender pink kind of algae. But today, because of the storm and resultant darkness, they all look a uniform sombre grey. A muffled peal of thunder penetrates down to Ichthyander's abode. He looks up.

There's a dark spot right above his head. Now what could that be? His lunch over he can go up and investigate. Gliding upward along the cliff-face he approaches the surface and sees a huge albatross rocking up and down, its orange-hued legs within a tempting reach. Up go his hands and close round the bird's legs. What fun! Bewildered the albatross unfolds its mighty wings in an upward rush, dragging Ichthyander clear. Once in the air Ichthyander's body regains weight and the albatross drops heavily down, covering him with its soft feathery breast. Ichthyander doesn't wait for the giant bird to start pecking his head, dives and the next moment breaks surface again some distance off. The albatross is winging its way out to sea and out of sight beyond the mountainous seas.

Ichthyander is floating on his back. The storm has passed by on its way to the east. Thunder rumbles, receding. Rain is pouring down in sheets. Ichthyander lies back, his eyes half-closed with exquisite pleasure. By and by he opens them, turns over and treads water for a better look round. He's on the crest of a colossal wave. Sky, ocean, wind, rain—all are one big wet whirl, roaring in its primordial fury. As if in impotent rage, little beards of foam tremble on the wavecrests and run in angry zigzags down their sides. What with the swell from the storm and the savage wind the mountains of seas pile one on top of the other and crash down to pile up again.

What strikes fear into the earthly man is great fun to Ichthyander. Of course, waves can be dangerous for him too, but, like a fish, he knows their ways. There are many kinds of waves. Some will toss you up and down, up and down, others will turn you feet first before you know where you are. He also knows what goes on under the waves, and how waves disappear when the wind has died down. It's the small waves that go first, then the big ones, but the dead swell stays for a long time afterwards. He delights in turning somersaults in the surf, though that isn't without its danger either. Once an extra big wave overturned him and threw him against a rock unconscious. That would have been the end for an ordinary human being, but Ichthyander came to in the water, only slightly the worse for the experience.

There is no rain any longer; it has shifted, as has the storm, eastwards. The wind has veered too, blowing in warm blasts from the tropical north. Heralded by patches of blue sky torn in the clouds, the sun thrusts its rays through—seawards. In the south-east across a still menacingly black sky a rainbow throws its double arc. It's an entirely different ocean that Ichthyander beholds now, no longer black with frothy fury, but a blue cheerful ocean, with emerald patches where sun rays have struck its breast.

The sun! In one moment it has changed everything—sky, ocean, shore, distant mountains—beyond recognition. And oh! How wonderful the air is after the storm. Ichthyander now gulps in the exhilarating sea-air, now breathes through his gills. No one knows better than Ichthyander how easy comes gill breathing after a storm has mixed sky with ocean, making the water a good deal richer in oxygen. No one, that is, among men.

But the numerous fish, and the sea-animals too, can appreciate this.

After a storm is over the sea depths, the crevices of the cliffs, the thickets of coral and sponge discharge their occupants; small fry show the way to the bigger fish and when it's quite calm again, to soft weak jellyfish, transparent, weightless shrimps, delicate *Porpita* and various *Ctenophora*, including the most beautiful representative of the group, the *Cestus Veneris*.

A sunray strikes the water close to Ichthyander, turning it a bright green. The glitter of tiny air bubbles, the hiss of foam. . . . Ichthyander's playmates, the dolphins, are gambolling nearby, throwing him gay, mischievous glances. Their shiny black backs flash into view in the waves as they chase one another playfully, snorting. Ichthyander laughs and joins in the game. He feels as though this ocean and these dolphins, the sky and sun, were all created expressly for him to enjoy.

Ichthyander raises his head and screws up his eyes at the sun. It is in the west of the sky. Evening is near. But today he doesn't feel like returning home early. He is going to rock on the waves until the first stars appear in the dark sky.

Yet lolling about soon tires him. And then, how could he forget all the small sea-creatures that are perishing that very moment. He treads water and looks in the direction of the distant shore. For the sand spit! That's where his help is really needed. There where the ocean surf is playing havoc.

After a storm it hurls ashore heaps of sea-weeds and sea-creatures, all kinds of fishes, crabs, jellyfish, starfish, sometimes even an unwary dolphin. Jellyfish soon perish but some of the fish manage to wriggle their way back. So do most of the crabs; in fact they themselves leave the water for the beach to prey on storm victims. And it does his heart good to come to their rescue.

For hours he roams the beach in search of what it is not too late to rescue. It gives him real pleasure to see a fish, thrown into the water, splash with its tail and swim away. Or, still more, to see a fish at first floating life-less side or belly up come at last to life. Picking up a large fish he will carry it seawards, pressing its wriggling body to his, laughing, as he talks to it in soothing accents. Of course, he would have eaten that very fish without any compunction had he been out in the ocean and hungry. But that's an evil of necessity. Here, on the beach, he is the sea-dwellers' patron, friend and saviour.

Usually Ichthyander returns home as he left—using the underwater current. But today he doesn't feel like going underwater for long, so beautiful are the ocean and sky. He dives, swims underwater and breaks surface again, not unlike a sea-bird hunting fish.

The last rays of sun are gone. The yellow band is dwindling in the western horizon. Gloomy waves like grey shadows chase one another.

Compared with the warm water the air has a nip in it. It's dark but Ichthyander feels safe; there's nobody to attack him at this hour of quiet that divides day and night.

* * *

Here is what he needs—the southbound current flowing quite close to the ocean's surface. The swell which is still felt makes the underwater river rise and fall a little as it traces its slow course from the hot north down to the cold south. A great deal lower—and in the opposite direction—runs a cold current.

Ichthyander makes good use of both of them when his trips take him along the coast.

The warm current will carry him all the way home. He only has to keep awake so as not to overshoot the tunnel-mouth as he once did. Stretching his arms behind his head and out to the side by way of exercise, and pulling his legs apart and slowly back together he lets himself be carried southwards. The warm water and slow movements have a soothing effect on him.

As Ichthyander looks up he sees a heaven dotted with stars as small as specks of dust. Those must be *Noctilucae*, rising to the ocean's surface with their tiny lanterns lit up. Here and there in the darkness he sees bluish and pinkish luminous nebulae—tight clusters of minute luminous animals. Balls emitting mild greenish light sail slowly by. Shedding light quite close to Ichthyander is a jellyfish looking for all the world like a lamp under an elaborate shade of lace with a long fringe. The fringe stirs as in a light breeze at every movement of the jellyfish. In the shallows starfish have already put on lights. In the depths below the lights of big fish of prey cruise at speed. They chase one another, circle, die out and flicker up afresh.

Another shallow. The bizarre trunks and

twigs of coral are illumined from within in blue, pink, green and white. Some corals flicker waningly, others gleam like red-hot metal.

On land at night you can see the stars, far off and tiny, sometimes the moon. Here there are thousands of stars, thousands of moons, thousands of small multicoloured suns all radiating soft delicate light. Night in the ocean is infinitely more beautiful than night on land.

To compare them Ichthyander breaks the surface again.

The air has become warmer. The dark blue heaven spread overhead is thickly studded with stars. A silver moon rides low above the horizon. A silver path runs from it across the ocean.

From off the harbour comes a low prolonged hoot. That is the giant *Horrocks*, getting ready for the return voyage. Hey, but it's late. Dawn is not far off. He has been gone nearly twenty-four hours. Father will definitely scold him.

Ichthyander heads for the tunnel, thrusts his hand through the iron bars, opens the grille and swims on in complete darkness. He is now in the lower, cold, current that runs from the sea to the garden ponds.

A light knock on his shoulder wakes him up. He's in the pool. Quickly he comes up;

starts breathing through his lungs, taking in the air fragrant with familiar flower scents.

A few minutes later he's fast asleep in bed—to please his father.

THE GIRL AND THE STRANGER

Once Ichthyander was out in the ocean after a storm.

Surfacing, he spotted what looked to him like a piece of white sail torn by the storm off some fishing smack. Coming nearer he realized to his surprise that it was a woman, or rather a young girl, tied to a board of wood. Was she dead? The thought so upset him that for the first time in his life a feeling of hostility towards the ocean stirred within him.

Or perhaps she was only unconscious? Holding up the girl's pretty head that was lolling to one side, Ichthyander grasped the board and pushed shorewards.

He swam for all he was worth, as he had never swum before, stopping only to see to the girl's head, which kept slipping off the board. And he kept whispering to her as he used to whisper to fish in trouble, "Wait a little, it'll soon be over." He wanted the girl to open her eyes and yet was afraid of it. He wanted her to come to life and yet was afraid she would get frightened. Had he not better take off his goggles and gloves? But that would take time and then he would not be able to make half as much progress with his gloves off. And so he pressed on, pushing the board with the girl closer and closer inshore.

At last he reached the heavy surf. Sharp was the word now. The waves were propelling him shorewards. Ichthyander kept feeling with his foot for a shallow place. Finally he struck bottom, safely steered his burden ashore, untied the girl and, laying her in the shade of a bush-grown dune, began administering artificial respiration.

He thought he saw her eyelids quiver, and putting his ear against the girl's heart he detected a faint beating. She was alive! He very nearly cried out with joy.

Then the girl half-opened her eyes, caught sight of Ichthyander and shuddered and shut her eyes again. Ichthyander was at once gladdened and chagrined. Well, anyway, I've saved the girl, he thought. Now he ought to be going away—to avoid frightening her. But could he leave her as she was now—all alone too? Even as he thought this he heard somebody's heavy footfalls. This was no time for indecision. Ichthyander ducked into a wave, swam underwater to the nearest reef, broke surface in its shelter and watched developments.

From behind the dune a swarthy man with a moustache and goatee showing from under a wide-brimmed hat swung into view. At the sight of the girl he exclaimed: *Gracias a Jesús y María!*", started to run towards her, then suddenly veered to the water's edge and into the oncoming wave. Thoroughly drenched he ran back towards the girl, started artificial respiration (whatever for, Ichthyander wondered); then bent low over the girl's face and kissed her. Presently he began speaking to her, rapidly and agitatedly. Snatches of phrases floated to Ichthyander: "I warned you ... it was sheer madness.... Good thing I thought of tying you to a board."

The girl opened her eyes and raised her head a little. Her face expressed fear, followed by surprise, then indignation and displeasure. The goateed man kept up a voluble flow of talk as he helped her up. But she was evidently still too weak and he eased her back onto the sand. Nor was it until about half an hour later that she could stand up again and walk. On their way they passed quite close to where Ichthyander was hiding. The girl was saying:

"So it was you who saved my life? Thank you. May God reward you for this."

"You alone can reward me," said the swarthy-skinned man.

The girl seemed not to hear the man's words.

"It's strange," she said after a pause. "I thought I saw a monster at my side."

"That was your imagination," the man said. "Or again it might have been the wicked one come to claim your soul. Say a prayer and lean on my arm—with me around you needn't be afraid of any devil."

And they were gone, the wonder girl and the evil man who was trying to make her believe it was he who had rescued her from the sea. But Ichthyander was in no position to give him the lie. Let him do as he liked; Ichthyander had done what he could.

The girl and her companion had disappeared behind the dunes but Ichthyander was still looking their way. Then he turned round and faced the ocean. How big it was—and how empty.

A wave had tossed a silver-bellied blue-backed fish on the sand. Ichthyander looked round him; not a soul in sight. He left his cover, retrieved the fish and threw it into the water. The fish swam away but Ichthyander felt sad without knowing why. For some time he wandered about the deserted beach, picking up fish and restoring them to their element. Gradually he was carried away by his work. Soon his usual high spirits were restored and, forgetting all about time, he pressed on, only breaking for an occasional plunge to cool his gills. It wasn't until quite dark that he finally turned for home.

ICHTHYANDER'S VALET

Salvator was going into the mountains again—this time without Cristo. Apparently well satisfied with Cristo's work, Salvator was leaving him behind to his now permanent duties of Ichthyander's servant. That suited Cristo's book for it would facilitate his meeting with Baltasar. Cristo had already sent word to him that he had discovered the "sea-devil's" whereabouts. It was time for them to lay plans for his kidnapping.

For some time now Cristo had been living in the white-stone lichen-covered cottage and seeing much of Ichthyander. Soon they had become good friends. Ichthyander, for whom human companionship was a welcome novelty, had fairly cottoned to the old Indian, who was so ready with tales about life on land—

something Ichthyander knew little about. But he knew more about life in the sea than the world's greatest experts on the subject all rolled in one. He had a good grounding in geography, at least as far as the oceans, seas and major rivers went; and also knew something of astronomy, navigation, physics, botany and zoology. But he knew little about men, actually nothing beyond the mere fact of the existence of different races on earth, something still vaguer about their history, and as to their political and economic relations, his knowledge did not exceed that of a five-year-old.

At noon when it grew hot Ichthyander would descend into the underground cave and swim away. He would return to the cottage when the heat had abated and stay there till the next morning. But if it rained or there was a storm at sea he would as often as not remain in the cottage the whole day and feel all right owing to the extra moisture.

The house was not big, just four rooms, one leading into another, and a kitchen. Cristo lived in the room next to the kitchen. Then came the dining-room and a big library (Ichthyander could read Spanish and English). The farthest and biggest room was Ichthyander's bedroom. A big bath took up most of its centre. The bed was on the side, against one of the walls, but Ichthyander seemed to prefer the bath to it. Before going away, however, Salvator had ordered Cristo to see to it that Ichthyander slept in his bed no less than three nights a week, and so every night Cristo saw Ichthyander to bed and grumbled like an old nurse if the young man was being disobedient.

"But I find it a good deal pleasanter sleeping in the water," protested Ichthyander.

"The Doctor's orders were that you should sleep in bed—you mustn't disobey your father."

Though Ichthyander called Salvator Father, the old Indian doubted they were blood relations at all. True, the amphibian's skin where it could be seen was rather pale, but that might be due to long immersions. Considering his elongated head, straight nose, thin lips and big sparkling eyes—Ichthyander rather struck Cristo as looking like an Araucanian.

Cristo wanted very much to see what colour Ichthyander's body was under its close-fitting suit made of some unknown material.

"Do you never take off this thing—not even for the night?" he asked the young man one evening.

"Why should I? I feel comfortable enough in it. It doesn't prevent either gill or skin breathing and besides is a good armour. Neither a shark's teeth nor a sharp knife can pierce it," Ichthyander replied.

"Why do you put goggles and those gloves and shoes on?" Cristo asked looking at the quaint objects lying near the bed. The gloves were made of greenish rubber and had extra finger joints with webs in between. The toes were still longer.

"The gloves and shoes are for faster swimming. And the goggles so that I don't get sand in my eyes. Besides I can see a good deal better with them on. Without goggles everything'd be lost in a fog down there." And smiling he continued, "When I was quite small Father used to let me play with the children in the other garden. I was very much surprised to see them swim without their gloves. 'How can you swim without gloves?' I asked them but they didn't understand what I meant, for I never swam in their presence."

"Do you still swim out into the gulf?" asked Cristo.

"Of course. Only I use the side tunnel. Some bad people nearly caught me with a net, so I'm very careful now."

"Hm. So there's a side tunnel leading to the sea, is there?"

"Yes, actually several of them. What a pity you can't go swimming with me. I could have shown you simply wonderful things. We'd have ridden my sea-horse together. Oh, why can't all people live underwater?"

"Your sea-horse? What's that?"

"It's a dolphin. I tamed him. I found the poor fellow on the shore after a storm, with a fin badly smashed. I dragged him into the water. That was quite a job, I can tell you. Dolphins weigh a lot more on land than they do in water. But then everything else does up here, in this world of yours. Even your own body. Life's easier down there, you know. So I dragged the dolphin into the water as I've said, but found he couldn't swim and that meant he couldn't get food either. I fed fish to him—for a whole month. In that time he not only became tame but sort of got attached to me. We made good friends. The other dolphins got to know me too. You can't imagine what great fun it is, gambolling in the waves with dolphins on a sunny day! It's good to be under the waves too. You seem to be swimming through thick blue air. It's quiet all round. You don't feel your own body; it becomes free, light, responsive to the merest movement. ... I have many friends out in the sea. I feed small fish as you'd feed birds, they follow me round in shoals."

"Haven't you any enemies?"

"Oh yes—sharks and octopuses. But I'm not afraid of them. I've got my knife."

"And what if they steal upon you unawares?"

Ichthyander looked surprised.

"Why, I can hear them coming at quite a distance."

"Hear them?" It was Cristo's turn to look surprised. "Even when they try to steal up on the sly?"

"That's right. Is there anything surprising? I can hear them with my ears and with my whole body. They make the water oscillate and the waves they produce run ahead of them. I feel them and so get my warning."

"Even when you're asleep?"

"Of course."

"But look, what about fishes?"

"Fish are beaten not by a surprise attack but by stronger fish. And I'm stronger than any of them. The fish of prey know it, too. They don't dare tackle *me*."

Zurita's right: the fellow's well worth the trouble of getting him, thought Cristo. And he'll take a lot of getting too. Hearing with his whole body! How do you like that? Nothing short of a damn good trap would get him for us. I must speak to Zurita about it.

"How beautiful the underwater world is!" Ichthyander was saying. "No, I'd never leave the sea for your stuffy dusty land."

"Why, isn't it yours too? You were born on land, weren't you? Who was your mother?"

"I–I don't know," Ichthyander stammered. "Father says my mother died giving me birth."

"But surely she was a mortal woman and not a fish."

"Perhaps," Ichthyander agreed.

Cristo gave a short laugh.

"Now tell me, why did you molest the fishermen, cutting their nets, throwing their catch back into the sea and all that?"

"Because they caught more than they could eat."

"But they caught fish to sell it."

Ichthyander did not understand.

"So that other people could eat fish too," the Indian had to explain.

"Why, are there so many people?" Ichthyander queried in surprise. "Haven't they got enough animals and birds on land? Why do they have to come to the ocean?"

"Ah, that's not so easy to explain," Cristo

said with a yawn. "It's time you were in bed, though. So don't you go crawling into the bathtub again. Your father will be displeased," and he went out.

Ichthyander was already gone when Cristo came in early next morning to find a little pool of water on the flagstones.

"Slept in the bathtub again, did he," the Indian said grumpily. "And then went out to sea."

Ichthyander was late for his breakfast that day.

He seemed upset over something, the way he poked about with his fork in the plate.

"Roast meat again," he said.

"That's right," Cristo said in a stern voice. "Those are Doctor's orders. Looks like you've been eating raw fish in the sea again. If this goes on much longer you'll not be able to touch roast meat, much less eat it. And you slept in the bathtub. You'll get that pain in the sides again, as sure as eggs is eggs. And now you're late for breakfast. When Doctor comes back I'll complain to him, see if I don't. Why, you've got quite out of hand lately."

"Don't tell him, Cristo. I don't want to make him sad." Ichthyander hung his head and was back in his thoughts. Then he suddenly raised his big, now melancholy, eyes at the Indian.

"Listen, Cristo," he said, "I saw a girl this morning. Never before have I seen anything nearly as beautiful—not even under the waves."

"So our land is not all that bad after all, eh?" said Cristo.

"I was riding my dolphin when I saw her on the beach near Buenos Aires. She had blue eyes and golden hair." And he added, "But when she saw me she got frightened and ran away. Oh, why didn't I take the goggles and gloves off?" After a pause he said in a low voice: "Once I pulled a girl out of the sea. I didn't notice then what she looked like. What if it's the same girl? I think I remember that one had golden hair too. Yes, I think she had. . . ." The young man was again lost in thought. Presently he went across to the mirror and for the first time in his life had a good look at himself.

"What did you do after she ran away?"

"I waited, but she never came back. Cristo, is it possible she will never come down to the beach again?"

Perhaps it's not at all bad that he likes the girl, Cristo thought. Up till now, praise the pleasures of the city as he would, he could not induce Ichthyander to venture as far as Buenos Aires, where his capture would have been no problem for Zurita.

"That's as may be, but I'll help you find her. You'll put on town clothes and we'll go and look for her in Buenos Aires."

"I will see her, won't I?" exclaimed Ichthyander.

"There're many girls there. With luck you'll find the one you saw on the beach."

"Let's go straightway! I'll ride my dolphin and you'll walk along the coast."

"It's too late. And it's not all that near on foot."

"Surely we can make it."

"Aren't you eager!" Cristo said. "We'll set out together at dawn tomorrow. You'll swim out into the gulf and I'll be waiting for you on the beach with the clothes. And I must get them for you first. (I'll have to call on my brother tonight, thought Cristo.) So see you at dawn."

IN TOWN

When Ichthyander waded out of the water onto the beach early next morning Cristo was already waiting for him with a white suit ready. Ichthyander looked at the suit as if it were a snake's skin and with a sigh started pulling it on. It was obvious he had had few occasions to dress in a suit before. The Indian helped the amphibian with his tie, looked him over and was pleased with what he saw.

"Let's go," he said cheerily.

The Indian wanted to impress Ichthyander, so he took him through the central streets, Avenida de Alvear and Plaza de Vertiz, on to Plaza de la Victoria with the Cathedral and the Town Hall in the Moorish style, then to Plaza del 25 de Mayo* with the Obelisco de la Libertad in the middle of a grove of magnificent trees, topping it all with the Palace of the President.

But Cristo's little scheme misfired. What with the noise, the never ending stream of city traffic, the heat and the crowds, Ichthyander was utterly bewildered and miserable. In vain he tried to find the girl in the crowd, grabbing Cristo by his arm every now and then and whispering, "That's her!" then realizing he was mistaken and again peering into the crowd.

About noon the heat became unbearable. Cristo suggested that they have lunch at a restaurant nearby. It was down in the basement, a cool place, but noisy and close and full of

---

* A revolutionary junta was formed in La Plata Province on May 25, 1810. Following a victorious uprising the province seceded from Spain and a provisional government was set up. – *Author's note.*

people in cheap soiled clothes, smoking foul cigars. The smoke made Ichthyander gasp for air. To make things worse the men were hotly discussing some piece of news, brandishing crumpled newspapers and bawling out words he didn't know. Ichthyander drank a lot of iced water but wouldn't touch his lunch.

"It's easier to find a fish in the ocean than a girl in this human whirlpool," he said sadly. "Your cities are beastly! They're stuffy and foul. And my sides are aching. I want to go back home, Cristo."

"All right," Cristo agreed. "We'll only drop in to see a friend of mine and then off we go back home."

"I don't want to see any more people."

"It's on our way. I won't be a minute."

Cristo paid their bill and they emerged into the sun-scorched street. Breathing heavily, his head hanging, Ichthyander plodded after the Indian past cactus-lined white-stone houses, past orchards with peach and olive trees onto Baltasar's place in the New Port.

With the tang of the sea ever stronger in his nostrils, Ichthyander wished, with a sudden vehemence, he could throw off his clothes and plunge into the water.

"We're nearly there," Cristo said glancing apprehensively at his companion.

They crossed a railway line.

"Here we are. This is the place," said Cristo and led the way down a few steps into a small dark shop.

When Ichthyander's eyes got used to the semi-darkness he gazed round him in surprise. The shop looked like a corner of the sea. The shelves and even part of the floor were piled high with every variety of shell. Hanging from the ceiling were strings of coral, starfish, dried-up crabs, and stuffed fish. There were pearls in glass cases arranged to form a counter. One of these displayed pink pearls, "angels' skin," as they are called by divers. Ichthyander felt more at ease amidst things he knew so well.

"Have a rest, it's cool and quiet down here," Cristo said helping the young man into an old wicker chair.

"Baltasar! Gutiérrez!" the Indian called.

"That you, Cristo?" a voice came from behind the door. "Come in here."

Cristo lowered his head to pass into the other room.

It was Baltasar's laboratory. It was here he restored to pearls the lustre they are apt to lose through dampness, by bathing them in a weak solution of acid. Cristo shut the door tight behind him. The dim light that filtered in through a small window high up a wall re-

107

vealed the flasks and glass tanks standing on an old deal table black with long use.

"Hullo, brother. Where's Gutiérrez?"

"Gone to the neighbour for the iron. Nothing but lace and ribbon on her mind. She'll be back any minute, though."

"And where's Zurita?" asked Cristo, impatiently.

"Hasn't shown up yet, damn his eyes. Had a bit of a row yesterday, we did."

"Over Gutiérrez?"

"Yes. He laid himself out to woo her. But she wouldn't have him. Now what can I do with her? She's no end wilful and stubborn. She is that. Thinks herself a cut above everybody else. She just can't understand that any Indian girl, fair or ugly, would jump at the idea of marrying a man like Zurita, with a schooner and a team of pearl-divers of his own," Baltasar grumbled, dumping a new batch of pearls into the tank. "He's somewhere trying to drown his annoyance in wine, I suppose."

"But what shall we do?"

"You brought him?"

"There he is."

Baltasar stepped to the door and bent down to the keyhole.

"I can't see him," he said softly.

"He's sitting over at the counter."

"I can't see him. There's only Gutiérrez there."

Baltasar flung the door open and entered the shop followed closely by Cristo.

Ichthyander was not there. In the dark corner stood Gutiérrez, Baltasar's adopted daughter, famed far beyond the New Port for her beauty. A shy girl with a head of her own, she had no lack of suitors but gave all of them her "no," firm and sonorous.

Pedro Zurita had cast his eye on her one day and wanted her ever since for his wife. And old Baltasar was not averse to become his father-in-law—and partner.

But all Zurita's advances met the same sonorous, firm "no."

When her father and Cristo came in the girl was standing still, her head drooping.

"Hullo, Gutiérrez," said Cristo.

"Where's the young man?" asked Baltasar.

"I don't hide young men," she said and smiled. "When I entered he looked at me in a funny way, as if afraid or something, rose up, then clutched at his chest and tore out. Before I knew it he was up the steps and gone."

So she was the girl, thought Cristo.

BACK IN THE SEA

Breathing in painful gasps Ichthyander ran along the road that skirted the sea-front. As soon as he was out of that dreadful city he left the road and headed straight for the beach. Taking shelter behind an outcropping of rock he peeled off his suit, hid it among the stones, ran to the water's edge and plunged in.

Exhausted as he was, he had never swum so quickly before. Fish scattered away out of his path in fright. It was only after he had put a few miles between himself and the city that he slowed down and turned closer inshore. Here he was at home. He knew every stone, every crevice on the sea-bed. Right below him spread flat on the sandy floor lived sedate turbot; over there grew red bushes of coral, a hiding place for small red-finned fish. Two families of octopuses shared that fishing boat wreck—and, incidentally, there had been a recent increase in their families, too. Those grey stones were the haunt of crabs. Ichthyander could watch them for hours, delighting in their small joys of a lucky hunt or sympathizing with their little griefs—of a nipper lost or an octopus invading. And the offshore rocks marked the breeding grounds of innumerable oysters.

When he was near the gulf he at last broke water and looked round. Seeing a school of dolphins gambolling among the waves he gave a shout. A large dolphin snorted gaily by way of acknowledgement and headed for his friend, his sleek, shiny back now disappearing in the waves, now rising above the surface again.

"Come on, Leading, be smart about it," Ichthyander was shouting as he swam out to meet the dolphin. Presently he had a hold of it, and without stopping, "Off we go!" he urged.

Obedient to the young man's guiding hand the dolphin turned for the open sea and dashed forward in the teeth of wind and waves. The animal churned the water as it cleaved its way through the waves and spread a fantail of foaming wash behind it, but Ichthyander was not to be satisfied. He kept urging his mount on.

"Come on, Leading, faster!"

The dolphin's sides were heaving heavily when Ichthyander put a sudden stop to the race, although still far from being his calmer self. He just slipped off the glistening back down into the water and was gone, leaving his friend behind in utter bewilderment. The dolphin waited a moment, snorted, dived and immediately reappeared, then gave another snort of displeasure, canted sharply and headed shorewards, glancing back from time to time. The amphibian was not to be seen anywhere, so Leading joined its school. Meanwhile Ichthyander was going deeper and deeper, down into the gloomy depths of the ocean. All that he had seen and heard that day was so unexpected, so beyond the beat of his experience, that he wanted to be alone. He was going deeper and deeper down, oblivious of the danger of it. He wanted to be alone to try and understand why he was so different from everybody else, why he was a stranger to both land and sea.

Then he slowed down his dive. The water had become denser, it pressed on him, making breathing increasingly difficult. A greyish-green pall cloaked everything around. Sea-creatures were fewer here and mostly unfamiliar to Ichthyander: he had never been so deep down before. And for the first time this silent murky world gripped Ichthyander's heart with terror. He went up as quickly as he could, broke water at last and swam shorewards. The sun was setting, its slanting, stark red shafts driving into the sea. Once in the water they blended with the blue of it into tender tones—from pinkish lilac to greenish blue.

As Ichthyander was not wearing his goggles the surface of the water from below looked to him as it looks to fish—not flat but cone-shaped, much as if he were at the apex of a huge funnel. The rims of the funnel seemed to be encircled by rings, red, yellow, green, blue and violet. Beyond these spread the bright surface of the water which reflected, mirror-like, the things below—rocks, weeds, fish.

Ichthyander turned face down, coasted along the bottom quite close inshore and squatted down among a group of underwater rocks near a shallow. The fishermen from a boat nearby jumped overboard to pull her clear. One of them stood in the water knee-deep. Ichthyander saw a legless fisherman above, and separately his legs below the water, duplicated in the mirror of the water's surface. Another fisherman got in shoulder-deep. And below the water a weird creature with no head but four legs suddenly reared up, looking like identical twins placed one on top of the other, shoulders to shoulders, their heads chopped off for a better fit. Whenever there were men wading out Ichthyander could always enjoy a good, fish's-eye view of them, full-length, but seen as in a glass ball, and swim away before they spotted him.

But today the strange bodies with four legs and no head, and the heads with no bodies to them looked definitely repulsive to Ichthyander. Men. . . . They were so noisy and smelly, they smoked such foul cigars. Yes, dolphins *were* better–the clean gay dolphins. Ichthyander grinned as he remembered how he had once tasted the dolphin's milk.

Way down to the south there was a small secluded cove. A belt of razor-sharp reefs and a great sandbank made access to it from the sea well-nigh impossible, while steep craggy cliffs cut it off from land. Neither fishermen nor pearl-divers visited the cove. Colourful marine growths thickly carpeted its shallow bottom. Small fish weaved to and fro in the warm water. For many years a she-dolphin had come here to bring forth her young, two, four or sometimes even six of them. Ichthyander found it great fun to watch the baby dolphins. For hours he would hide among the rocks and watch them romp in the waves or rush back to their mother to nudge their way to her nipples. Then Ichthyander started to tame them little by little, treating them to small fish. By and by the baby dolphins and their mother got used to him. The little fellows didn't mind him chasing them, catching them, tossing them in the air. Indeed they seemed to like it—they wouldn't leave his side and flocked to him from afar as soon as he appeared in the cove, his hands full of titbits—fish or, still better, small octopuses.

One day when the dolphin he already knew had just had her young and they ate no fish yet but only drank their mother's milk, Ichthyander thought why he himself shouldn't taste it.

The next moment he was under the dolphin, clutching at her and pressing his mouth to a nipple. The creature, only a moment ago absolutely carefree, now rushed off horror-stricken. Ichthyander let go of her at once. The milk had tasted strongly of fish.

Rid of her unwelcome suckling, the terrified dolphin went right out of the cove while her young stayed behind, dashing here and there, also terrified and bewildered. It took Ichthyander some time and effort to round up the silly little dolphins. By the time he had them all together the mother was back for her young and took them to a cove nearby. It wasn't until days later that he won back the family's trust.

*   *   *

Cristo was nearly off his head with worry. Ichthyander had been gone for three days and nights when at last he appeared, his face thin and tired, but relaxed.

"Now, where've you been hiding yourself?" the Indian inquired in a stern voice, overjoyed though he was to see Ichthyander back.

"On the sea-bottom," Ichthyander replied.

"Why are you so pale?"

"I—I nearly lost my life," Ichthyander told his first lie and started on the story of an adventure that had happened to him quite some time before.

There was a rocky plateau out in the ocean with a big oval hollow in the middle of it, looking exactly like a submarine mountain lake.

Swimming over it one day Ichthyander was struck by the extraordinary light grey of its bottom. Going deep, he was amazed to find that the hollow was nothing else than a vast cemetery of sea-creatures—from small fish to sharks and dolphins. Some of them seemed recent additions but, strangely enough, no preying carrion-eaters were to be seen anywhere. The scene was one of death and quiet unchallenged. Only here and there tiny bubbles of gas would escape and trace their way up. Ichthyander was swimming above the rim of the hollow, when he was prompted to go still a little deeper. Suddenly sharp pain seared his gills and he fell in a helpless heap, all but unconscious, onto the rim of the hollow. He lay there, his heart racing wildly, a ceaseless pounding in his temples. It was the end. Then through the red mist in his eyes he saw a shark, its body writhing, falling into the hollow only a few feet away. It must have been stalking him until it too had come into contact with the deadly water of the submarine lake. Its belly and sides heaved and fell, its mouth gaped open, baring the sharp white plates of its teeth. The beast was dying. Ichthyander shuddered. His teeth set in a supreme effort, trying to keep water out of his gills, Ichthyander crawled away from the fatal spot on all fours, then struggled up to his feet and lurched on. He felt dizzy and fell to the ground again. Then he pushed off it, struck out with his arms and there he was at last, a dozen paces from the hollow and swimming desperately away.

To round off the story Ichthyander added for Cristo's benefit what he had subsequently learned from Salvator.

"Some harmful gas, hydrogen sulphide or carbon anhydride, has accumulated over the years there, most likely," Ichthyander said.

"You see when it reaches the surface it's already oxidized and no longer harmful but in the hollow it's highly concentrated. Well, I could do with a bit of breakfast now—I'm fairly famished."

After a hasty meal Ichthyander grabbed his goggles and gloves and made straight for the door.

"What, have you only come back to get those? " Cristo said, pointing at the goggles. "What's the matter with you? Why don't you tell me?"

But Ichthyander was no longer his open-hearted self.

"Don't ask me, Cristo. I don't know myself what's the matter with me," he said and hurried out.

REVENGE IS SWEET

Ichthyander had been so shaken at the sudden appearance of the girl that he had just rushed out of Baltasar's shop and never stopped until he was in the sea swimming away. Now he was dying to see her but he did not know how to go about it. The easiest thing would be to enlist Cristo's help. But he was afraid that might involve speaking to her in the Indian's presence. Every morning Ichthyander would swim to where he had first seen her on the beach and stay there till evening, hiding among some boulders, in the hope of seeing her. On coming ashore, he took off his goggles and gloves and donned his white suit lest the girl should get frightened again. Sometimes, his vigil over, he would dine on fish and oysters, spend a restless night in the coastal waters and be back at his post before dawn broke.

One evening he resolved to go to Baltasar's shop. The door was open. But he could only see the old Indian behind the counter. Ichthyander was making his way back when high on a rocky headland he saw a girl in a light white dress and a straw hat. That was her. Ichthyander halted, not daring to go nearer. The girl was apparently waiting for somebody. She was pacing the rocky platform impatiently, throwing a glance now and then at the road. She didn't see Ichthyander standing below at the foot.

Then the girl waved to somebody. Ichthyander turned and saw a tall, broad-shouldered young man, coming briskly along the road. Never before had Ichthyander seen such light hair and eyes as the stranger's. The young giant walked up to the girl and offered her his broad hand.

"Hullo, Gutiérrez, dear," he said tenderly.

"Hullo, Olsen."

The stranger gave Gutiérrez's hand a good shake.

Ichthyander eyed him with an ill-feeling tinged with sadness.

"Brought it?" the young man said.

She merely nodded.

"Will your father not notice?" asked Olsen.

"No," she said. "Anyway the pearls are mine. I can do with them as I please."

Speaking in undertones Gutiérrez and Olsen walked to the very edge of the cliff. Presently Gutiérrez unlocked her necklace and held it up by one end.

"Look, how beautifully the pearls play in the setting sun," she said admiringly. "Here, take it."

But even as Olsen stretched out his hand the necklace slipped out of Gutiérrez's hand and plummeted into the sea.

"Oh, what have I done!" cried the girl.

Both stood rooted to the spot in their dismay.

"Perhaps it can be recovered?" said Olsen.

"No, the water's far too deep here," Gutiérrez said. "Oh, isn't that terrible!"

Seeing the girl so upset, Ichthyander forgot all about her having intended to make a present of the necklace to that fair-haired stranger. He just couldn't remain a mere witness any longer. With a determined step he went up and across to where Gutiérrez was standing.

Olsen frowned while Gutiérrez looked at Ichthyander with curiosity and surprise—she immediately recognized him as the young man who had left her father's shop the other day so abruptly.

"I gather you've dropped a pearl necklace into the sea?" he said. "I'll get it for you if you want me to."

"Even my father couldn't do it, not here, and he's one of the best pearl-divers there are," the girl retorted.

"I can only try," Ichthyander said modestly and, to their surprise, he dived right from where they stood, fully clothed as he was, and disappeared in the waves.

Olsen didn't know what to think.

"Who's that? Where did he spring from?"

A minute passed, then another but there was no sign of the young man.

"He's killed himself," Gutiérrez said, peering anxiously into the waves.

Ichthyander had not meant the girl, or Olsen for that matter, to know that he could live below the water. But carried away by the search he lost count of time and over-stayed an ordinary diver's performance. Coming to the surface he smiled and said, "A little patience. The place's cluttered up with broken rock. But I'll find it," and dived back.

Gutiérrez knew enough of pearl-diving to be surprised at seeing a man, just back from a two-minute deep dive, breathing evenly and looking so fresh.

In another two minutes his head popped into sight again. He was beaming all over his face as he lifted up a hand to show the necklace.

"It was caught on a crag," he shouted and his breathing was as even as if it had been the next room he had fetched the necklace from. "Wouldn't have been half as easy had it fallen into a crevice."

He scrambled quickly up the rocks, went to Gutiérrez and handed her the necklace. Water sluiced down his clothes—unheeded.

"Here you are."

"Thank you very much," Gutiérrez said and looked at Ichthyander with renewed curiosity.

A pause ensued. None of them knew what to do next. Gutiérrez seemed hesitant to pass the necklace to Olsen in Ichthyander's presence.

"I gather you wanted to give the pearls to him," Ichthyander said, pointing at Olsen.

Olsen reddened.

"Oh yes,—yes," Gutiérrez said in embarrassment and held out her hand to Olsen who took the necklace and slipped it into his pocket without saying a word.

Ichthyander was pleased with his little revenge. Olsen had received the lost necklace from Gutiérrez's hand, yes, but it was he, Ichthyander, who had got it for him.

And, bowing to the girl, Ichthyander strode quickly away along the road.

But his pleasant feeling was short-lived. New puzzling questions were battering for answer in his brain. Who was that fair-haired giant of a man? Why should Gutiérrez make him a present of her necklace? What was it they spoke about up there on the cliff-top?

That night again Ichthyander raced astride his dolphin through the waves, striking terror into the fishermen by his weird cries.

The whole of the next day Ichthyander spent below the water, goggled but gloveless, crawling along the sandy bottom in search of pearl-shells. In the evening he came back, to the grumbling of Cristo. Early the next morning he was at the rock where Gutiérrez and Olsen had had their rendezvous. Gutiérrez came in the evening, when the sun was already setting.

Ichthyander left his shelter to meet her. On seeing him Gutiérrez nodded by way of greeting.

"You are following me, aren't you?" she said with a smile.

"Yes," Ichthyander said simply, "ever since I first saw you," and, flushing with embarrassment, he went on, "You gave your necklace away to that . . . to Olsen. But you'd looked at it in an admiring way before you gave it to him. Do you like pearls?"

"Yes."

"Well then, take this . . . from me," and he held out a pearl.

Gutiérrez knew a first-rate pearl when she saw one. But the pearl that was glowing in Ichthyander's palm far excelled any pearl she had seen or heard her father speak about; enormous, exquisitely shaped, of the purest white, it must have weighed at least two hundred carats and been worth every bit of a million gold *pesos*. Astounded, Gutiérrez shifted her glance from the superb gem to the good-looking young man who was holding it out to her. Strong and lithe but somewhat shy, wearing a crumpled white suit, he did not look like one of the wealthy young *porteños*. And here he was offering her, a girl he hardly knew at all, such a present.

"Do take it—please," Ichthyander insisted.

"No," Gutiérrez said, shaking her head. "I cannot accept from you such a valuable present."

"Valuable!" Ichthyander rejoined hotly. "Why, there are thousands of pearls like this on the sea-bottom."

Gutiérrez smiled. Ichthyander once more felt embarrassed and was silent for a moment.

"Please," he said.

"No."

Ichthyander frowned. Now he felt offended.

"If you don't want to take it for yourself, then take it for Olsen. *He* won't refuse."

Gutiérrez was angry.

"It wasn't for himself he took it," she said in a severe tone of voice. "You don't know anything."

"So it's no, is it?"

"No."

Then Ichthyander threw the pearl far out into the sea, and with a curt nod turned round on his heels and went down to the road.

What he had done left Gutiérrez dumbstruck. To throw a million-worth fortune into the sea, just like a pebble picked up from the beach! She felt ashamed too, and scolded herself for being so heartless as to hurt that strange young man's feelings.

"Wait, where're you going?"

But Ichthyander was going away, his head
bowed. Then Gutiérrez caught up with him,
took him by his hand and looked into his
face. Tears were running down the young
man's cheeks. He had never wept before and
was wondering why everything round looked
blurred as if he were swimming underwater
with no goggles on.

"Please forgive me. I didn't mean to hurt
you," the girl said and took him by both his
hands.

THE IMPATIENCE OF ZURITA

After this event Ichthyander swam every
evening to the shore near the city, walked to
the place where he hid his suit, put it on and
went to the headland to meet Gutiérrez. Together they strolled along the shore, talking
animatedly. Who was Gutiérrez's new friend?
She wouldn't have been able to answer that.
He was intelligent and witty and knew many
things she did not know and yet, sometimes,
he did not understand things a schoolboy
would not need to think twice about. This
she could not explain. Ichthyander did not
speak about himself much. He shrank from
telling her the whole truth. What the girl

gathered was that Ichthyander was the son of a doctor, apparently a man of great means. He had brought up his son away from cities and people and had given him a peculiar one-sided education.

Sometimes they sat for long hours on the beach, close to the soughing sea. The stars would twinkle to them from the sky. By and by their conversation would die down. Ichthyander was happy.

"It's time I was going back," the girl would say.

Reluctantly Ichthyander rose, saw her as far as the suburb, returned quickly, threw off his suit and swam all the way home. In the morning, after his breakfast, he would swim out into the gulf, taking along with him a large loaf of bread. Settling down comfortably on the sandy bottom he would start feeding crumbs to the fish. They would come by shoals, swarming about him, slip in and out between his hands and snap up the sodden crumbs greedily. Sometimes bigger fish would gatecrash and chase the small fry. Ichthyander rose and shooed the brutes away while the small fish took shelter behind his back.

He also did some pearl collecting, which he found he liked. He was on top of the job in no time and soon had quite a pile of first-rate pearls in a corner of the underground cave that he used as a store.

He was fast becoming—quite unaware of it—one of the richest men in Argentina, perhaps even in the whole of Latin America. Had he only wanted, he could have easily become the richest man in the world. But this was farthest from his thoughts.

So passed quiet days. The only thing that clouded his happiness was her having to live in that stuffy city, full of dust and noise. What wouldn't he give to make it possible for her to live underwater, away from people and the noise they make. How wonderful that would have been! He would have shown her a new universe, walked with her through the flower-decked submarine fields. But she could not live underwater. Neither could he on land. As it was he was spending on land much more time than was useful for him. He was already paying for it: the pain in his sides grew with each day spent on the beach. But even when the pain became almost unbearable he never went away first. And then there was another source of worry. Do what he might he could not forget that whispered conversation Gutiérrez and the fair-haired stranger had had on the cliff-top. Each time Ichthyander meant to ask her and each time he didn't, afraid lest he should offend her.

One evening the girl told him that she was not coming the next day.

"Why?" he asked, and frowned.

"I'll be busy."

"What with?"

"You mustn't be so inquisitive," the girl said with a smile. "And don't see me off," she added and went away.

Ichthyander sank into the sea. All the night through he lay on a bed of moss-grown stones, feeling utterly miserable. At the first streak of day he headed for home.

When he was near the gulf he saw some fishermen dolphin-hunting. Under his very eyes a big dolphin, hit by a bullet, jumped high out of the water and splashed heavily back.

"Leading!" Ichthyander whispered in horror.

One of the fishermen was already in the sea, treading water, waiting for the wounded beast to surface. But the dolphin came up half a cable away, gasped for air and was down again.

As the fisherman was swiftly swimming to intercept his quarry, Ichthyander rushed to his friend's rescue. The dolphin came up again.

The next moment the fisherman was on it, and dragging it by its fin towards the coming boat.

Spurting on just under the waves, Ichthyander caught up with the fisherman and sunk his teeth into his calf. The fisherman gave a few violent jerks, no doubt sure he was attacked by a shark, and then slashed out blindly with the knife he had in his hand. The knife caught Ichthyander on part of the neck not protected by his mailcoat. He let go of the fisherman's leg and the latter went frantically for the boat. Ichthyander and the dolphin, both wounded now, headed for the gulf. The amphibian ordered the dolphin to follow him and dived into the underwater cave. It was only half-filled with water. Air got in through the fissured rock. Here he could examine the dolphin's wound in complete safety. It proved nothing serious. The bullet was lodged in the layer of fat. After working on it a little he was able to extract it with his bare hands. The dolphin had been remarkably patient throughout.

"There, it'll heal in no time," Ichthyander said, patting his friend's back lovingly.

Now he could look after himself. Ichthyander swam along the underwater tunnel, emerged in the orchard and entered his cottage.

Cristo was alarmed, seeing his ward wounded.

"What's happened?"

"Some fishermen wounded me when I was rescuing the dolphin," Ichthyander said. But Cristo did not believe him.

"Been to town again, on your own, haven't you?" he asked suspiciously, as he bandaged the wound. Ichthyander was silent.

"Pull your scales aside a little," Cristo said and exposed part of Ichthyander's shoulder. There was a red spot on it.

That added to Cristo's alarm.

"Did they strike you with an oar?" he asked, kneading the shoulder. But nothing seemed wrong with it. The spot looked like a birthmark.

"No," said Ichthyander.

Then the young man went to his room to have a rest while the old Indian sat down to do some thinking. After quite a time he got up and went out.

Cristo left for town. By the time he had reached Baltasar's shop he was quite out of breath. He entered and looked closely at Gutiérrez sitting behind the counter.

"Father home?" he asked.

"In there," the girl said, pointing with her chin at the other room.

Cristo went into Baltasar's laboratory and shut the door behind him.

He found his brother at work, in a bad mood again.

"It's enough to drive one mad, all your carryings-on," Baltasar was grumbling. "Zurita's as angry as a nest of vipers at you dilly-dallying with that 'sea-devil' fellow, Gutiérrez's cut somewhere for whole days. And she won't hear about Zurita. Keeps saying no. And Zurita says he's had enough of it. 'I'll carry her off by force,' he says. 'She'll weep a bit and then come round,' he says. And you can expect anything from him, damn his eyes."

Cristo listened to his brother's tale of woe in silence.

"Look," he said at last, "I couldn't bring Ichthyander here because he wouldn't come to town with me. He too has been out every day lately. Got quite out of hand. I'll catch it hot from Doctor for not looking after Ichthyander properly—"

"That means we've got to get hold of Ichthyander before Salvator arrives, then you can clear out and—"

"Wait a minute, Baltasar. Don't interrupt me. Listen. We mustn't rush things with Ichthyander."

"Why?"

Cristo sighed as if not quite prepared to say what was on his mind.

"You see—" he began.

But at that very moment somebody entered the shop and they heard Zurita's loud voice.

"There you are," Baltasar muttered, dumping a batch of pearls into the bath. "Him again."

Zurita dashed the door open and strode in.

"Ah, here's the precious pair. Well, now, when are you going to stop playing your damned tricks on me?" he said, looking from Baltasar to Cristo.

"I'm doing my best," Cristo said, rising and smiling politely. "Have a little patience, master. The 'sea-devil's' no small fry. You can't hook him up just like that. I brought him to town once, didn't I, but you were away, so he had a look round, didn't like what he saw and there you are—he won't be coaxed into coming again."

"Well, he can damn well please himself. I've done enough waiting, anyway. I'm pulling off two things at one stroke this week. Salvator still away?"

"He's expected any day now."

"That means we must hurry. You're going to have guests, Cristo,—a hand-picked bunch. You will open the doors for us, I'll see to the rest. I'll let Baltasar know when everything's ready," and, turning to Baltasar, he said, "As for you, we're going to have a talk tomorrow. Our last, mark you."

The two brothers bowed to him in silence. But as soon as Zurita turned his back on them to leave, gone were the polite smiles from their faces. Baltasar swore under his breath. Cristo seemed to be pondering something.

Out in the shop Zurita was saying something softly to Gutiérrez.

"No!" the two brothers heard her answer

Baltasar shook his head in dejection.

"Hey, Cristo!" called Zurita. "Come along, you'll be needed today."

AN UNPLEASANT ENCOUNTER

Ichthyander was in a very poor state indeed. His wound was still giving him pain, he was running a high temperature and was finding it hard to breathe with his lungs

But despite all this he had come to the rocks in the morning to meet Gutiérrez. She came at noon, when the heat was overpowering. What with hot air and fine white dust, Ichthyander was breathing in gasps. He wanted Gutiérrez to stay with him on the sea-shore, but she was in a hurry to go back.

"Father's going away on business, so he wants me to stay in the shop," she said.

"I will see you off then," he said and they set out townward along the hot dusty road.

Coming towards them, his head bent, was Olsen. Apparently preoccupied with something he drew level and would have gone past them, had not the girl hailed him.

"I must have a few words with him," Gutiérrez said to Ichthyander and then joined Olsen. They spoke in rapid undertones. The girl seemed to be trying to talk him into something.

Ichthyander stood waiting a few paces away.

"Well then, see you round midnight," he heard Olsen's voice. He shook the girl's hand and quickly went his way.

When Gutiérrez came back to Ichthyander's side his face was flushed. He was on the point of speaking to her about Olsen but still could not find words.

"I can't bear it," he began, gasping for air, "I must know... Olsen ... you're hiding something from me. You're going to meet him tonight, aren't you? Do you love him?"

Gutiérrez took Ichthyander by his hand and looked at him gently.

"Do you trust me?" she said.

"I do ... you know I love you," he had found the word at last, "but I ... but I'm suffering. . . ."

And he was too. He was suffering because of uncertainty and because at that moment a cruel pain was racking his sides. He was struggling for breath. The colour had drained from his cheeks.

"You look quite ill," the girl said in an anxious tone. "Do try and take yourself in hand. My dear boy, I didn't want to tell you everything but to set your heart at rest I will. Listen to me."

A man on horseback rushed past, then veered sharply round and rode up to the young couple. Ichthyander looked up and saw a swarthy man no longer in his youth with a pointed moustache and goatee.

He was sure he had seen the man some time, sowewhere. In town? No. Yes, that time on the shore!

The horseman was tapping his shiny boot with the riding crop as he gave Ichthyander a vile look and then held his hand out to Gutiérrez.

Grasping her hand, he suddenly lifted it up to kiss.

"Caught you!" he guffawed and releasing the hand of the frowning Gutiérrez, he went on in a bantering voice edged with truculence. "Now is it at all seemly for a young bride to be walking about with a young man just on the eve of her wedding?"

Gutiérrez flushed in anger but he did not give her time to speak.

"Father's been waiting for you. I'll be back there in an hour's time."

Ichthyander did not hear the last words. All of a sudden everything had gone dark in front of his eyes, there was a lump in his throat, his breathing had nearly stopped. He felt he could no longer stay on land.

"So you . . . after all . . . were deceiving me," he managed to utter with lips that had turned blue. He wanted to speak, to voice his indignation, to find out the whole truth, but the pain in his sides was so unbearably acute that he suddenly knew he was going to lose consciousness.

Ichthyander tore away towards the sea and dropped into the water from the cliff-top.

Gutiérrez cried out and staggered. Then she rushed to Pedro Zurita.

"Quick, save him!"

But Zurita did not budge.

"It's not in my habit to interfere with someone who wants to drown himself," he said smugly.

Gutiérrez ran seawards. It looked as if she, too, wanted to throw herself into the sea. Zurita dug his heels into his horse, caught up with the girl, seized her by the shoulders, lifted her up onto the saddle and galloped off along the road.

"It's not my habit to interfere with those who do not interfere with me. It's better that way. Try and be sensible, Gutiérrez."

Gutiérrez never said a word. She had fainted. It was only at her father's shop that she at last came to.

"Who was that young man?" Pedro asked.

Gutiérrez looked at Zurita with a loathing she did not want to disguise.

"Let me go," she said.

Zurita frowned. Well, nothing in it, probably, he thought. And then her hero has jumped into the sea. Couldn't do better. And turning to the shop he shouted, "Hey, Baltasar!"

Baltasar ran out.

"Here, take your daughter. And thank me that you're seeing her at all. I saved her—she nearly jumped into the sea after a young man with plenty of good looks. This is the second time I've saved your daughter's life and she's still shy in my company. Well, I'm going to see it stops soon." He guffawed. "Be back in an hour. Remember our deal!"

Baltasar was bowing servilely.

Zurita spurred his horse on and galloped away.

Father and daughter entered the shop. Gutiérrez sank onto a stool and buried her face in her hands.

Baltasar shut the door and, pacing the floor, began speaking in an agitated manner. But nobody was listening to him. He might just as well have been speaking to the dried-up crabs and half-moons lying on the shelves.

He's jumped into the sea, the poor boy, the girl thought, Ichthyander's face floating in front of her mind's eye. First Olsen, then that stupid encounter with Zurita. How dared he call me a bride. Everything is lost. . . .

Gutiérrez wept. She was sorry for Ichthyander. Simple and shy, he was a cut above all those vain and arrogant young men she had seen in the city.

What shall I do? she thought. Throw myself into the sea like Ichthyander? Put an end to it all?

Baltasar was saying:

"Do you understand what it means, Gutiérrez? It means ruin. Everything you see in this shop belongs to Zurita. What belongs to me won't make up one-tenth of it. All my pearls I receive from Zurita on commission. He's got me where he wants me. If you turn him down this time he'll take away what's his and stop doing business with me. And that means ruin. Complete ruin. Be a good girl, pity your old father."

"Go on, why don't you say, 'and marry him.' But I won't!" Gutiérrez said sharply.

"To hell with it!" cried Baltasar, his blood up. "In that case I . . . Zurita himself will make you do it!" And the old Indian went into his laboratory, slamming the door shut behind him.

FIGHTING OCTOPUSES

Once in the sea Ichthyander forced himself to forget all the misfortunes that had befallen him on land. After the hot and dusty land the cool water was all the more refreshing and soothing. The shooting pains ceased. His breathing was once again deep and even. What he wanted now was to relax and forget.

But Ichthyander had an active disposition. Idleness could not help him to forget. He tried to think of something to do. On dark nights he was fond of diving from a high cliff, deep enough to touch the bottom. But it was just past midday and above his head black bottoms of fishing boats were tracing their courses in the water.

"I know what I'll do. I'll put the cave in order," Ichthyander told himself.

In the sheer wall of a cliff in the gulf there was a cave with a finely arched entrance, giving a grandstand view of the submarine plain gently sloping into the ocean depths. For long Ichthyander had had an admiring eye for the spot. But to settle in it he had first to oust its lawful occupants—numerous families of octopuses.

Armed with his long slightly curved knife Ichthyander swam up to the cave and stopped at the mouth, not daring to enter. Then he thought he would tease the enemy into the open. From his previous visits he remembered seeing a long harpoon lying near a capsized boat close by. Finding it he took up his position at the cave-mouth and began poking about in it. The octopuses came to life, indignant at the intrusion. Tentacles crept into view in the archway. Gingerly they approached the harpoon but Ichthyander snatched it away before they could get a good hold on it. The play went on for a few minutes, until dozens of tentacles were writhing and swaying like a snaky-headed Gorgon in the archway. At last an enormous old octopus whose patience had

141

snapped decided to teach the cheeky intruder a lesson. It squeezed itself outside and moving its tentacles in a threatening way and changing its colour slowly bore down upon the enemy. Ichthyander swam to the side, dropped his harpoon and braced himself for battle. He knew full well from experience that man with his two arms stands little chance in fighting an octopus with its eight long powerful tentacles unless he goes straight for its body. So he let the octopus come quite near, then suddenly lunged forward, into the very centre of the tangle of tentacles, close to the mollusc's parrot-like beak.

This always catches an octopus unawares. And as always it took this octopus no less than four seconds to bring the tips of its tentacles in. But by that time Ichthyander had already, in a single swift unerring movement, slashed the beast's body in two, severing its motor nerves. And the huge tentacles, already all round him, went limp and dropped down.

"That's one."

He picked up his harpoon again. This time two octopuses swam out, one of them coming straight to tackle Ichthyander while the other tried to outflank him and attack him from the rear. Things were taking a more dangerous turn. Undaunted, however, Ichthyander attacked the octopus in front of him but before he was through with it the other one had a tentacle round his neck. The young man swiftly cut it off at his very neck, turned round and started to hack off the other tentacles. When, at last, the mutilated octopus was dropping slowly to the bottom Ichthyander returned to the first and finished it off.

"Three," Ichthyander counted.

But now he had to beat a temporary retreat A whole troop of octopuses had emerged from the cave-mouth, barely visible in the bloodstained water. In that brown murky haze the odds would be heavy against him, for the enemy could easily find him by touch. He swam a little way off, to the clear water, and killed there a fourth octopus which had unwisely ventured outside the bloody cloud.

The battle lasted on and off for several hours.

When finally the last octopus had been killed and the water had cleared Ichthyander saw numerous dead bodies and severed tentacles still writhing all round him. He then entered the cave. A few small octopuses were still there—the size of a fist, with tentacles no thicker than his finger. Ichthyander wanted to kill them off but then felt sorry for them.

I'll try and tame them, he thought. Couldn't find better guards for the place.

The question of guarding the place settled, Ichthyander went over to fixing up his new abode with some furniture. From his cottage he fetched a marble-topped table with four sturdy iron legs and two Chinese vases. He placed the table in the middle of the cave, put the vases on it, filled them with earth and planted some marine flowers. Some of the earth was washed away and writhed up in two columns of smoke for some time, then the water cleared. Only the flowers went on swaying slightly as if stirred by a gentle breeze.

There was a ledge in one of the walls, a sort of natural stone bench. The new master of the cave stretched himself out on it and looked with approval at the result of his labours. Under water the stone bench felt quite soft.

It was a strange submarine room with a table and two Chinese vases on it. Numerous curious fish came to attend the queer house-warming. They darted in and out between the table legs, swam to the flowers in the vases as if for an appreciative sniff and even whisked between Ichthyander's head and the arm on which it rested. A marble bullhead looked in at the entrance, waved its tail in puzzled alarm and swam off. A large crab crawled in across the white sand, raised and lowered a pincer as if saluting the master of the house and settled down under the table.

Ichthyander was finding it all great fun. As he lay there he thought of more things to beautify his new home with. "Out at the entrance I'll plant the most beautiful marine flowers there are. I'll strew the floor with pearls and place shells at the foot of the walls. If only Gutiérrez could see my submarine room. But she's deceiving me. Or is she? After all she wanted to tell me something about Olsen but had no chance to." Ichthyander frowned.

Then the stillness of the place began to crowd in on him. He felt alone again. Why can't people live underwater like me? he thought. I wish Father had come back. I'll ask him.

He wanted to show his new home to somebody. Anybody. Suddenly he remembered Leading. Good old Leading!

Ichthyander took up his winding shell, surfaced and blew through it. Soon he could hear the familiar snorting.

When the dolphin had joined him, Ichthyander embraced his friend.

"Come with me, Leading," he said, "I'll show you my new home. And you've never before

seen a table or a Chinese vase." Then, ordering the dolphin to follow him, he dived down.

But the dolphin turned out to be a trouble-
some guest. Big and awkward, it raised such a
commotion in the cave that the vases tottered
and all but fell down. Then it managed to
brush a leg of the table with its nose, overturning the table and sending the vases to the
floor. On land that would have been the end
of them, here nothing had happened, save for
the frightened crab, which scurried out side-
wise with an amazing speed.

"How awkward you are," Ichthyander said
as he pushed the table to the back of the cave
and picked up the vases.

Then he went to the dolphin's side and put
both his arms round him.

"Stay with me here, Leading," he said.

But soon the dolphin began shaking its
head and showing other signs of unrest. It
could not stay underwater for long spells. It
needed air. So with one powerful thrust of its
fins the dolphin swam outside and up to the
surface.

Even Leading can't live with me underwater, Ichthyander thought sadly, alone again.
Only fish, but they are shy and silly.

And he sank back on his stone couch. The
sun had set; it was dark in the cave. The

water in it rose and fell a little with a soothing effect.

Soon, tired with the day's excitement and
work, Ichthyander was lulled to sleep.

A NEW FRIEND

Olsen was on board a big launch, looking
over the rail into the water. The sun had just
risen but it was already high enough for its
slanting rays to pierce like blue-tinted searchlights to the very bottom of the shallow cove.
A few Indians were crawling over the white-
sand sea-floor. Every now and then they came
up for a good breath of air and then plunged
back. Olsen kept an eye on them. It was hot,
in spite of the early hour. By and by he felt
he could do with a dip or two, undressed
quickly and dived overboard. Olsen had never
done any pearl-diving before but he soon
found that he could stay underwater longer
than the professionals. So he joined the divers,
thrilled to be doing something that was quite
new to him.

Back at the bottom for a third time Olsen
saw two Indians, working side by side, suddenly jump up and swim desperately to the
surface as if a pack of sharks or sawfish were
after them. Olsen fronted round. Swiftly com-

ing to him with strong frog-wise thrusts was a
queer silver-scaled creature, half-man, half-
frog, with enormous bulging eyes and webbed
paws.

Before Olsen had time to rise from his knees
the monster was near him and holding him by
his arm with its frog-like paw. Scared as he
was Olsen realized that the creature had a
human face, whose good looks were only
marred by a pair of bulging glittering eyes.
The queer creature, apparently forgetting all
about being underwater, began speaking to
him. Olsen could not hear a word. He only
saw lips moving in speech. With its two front
paws the creature had a tight grip on Olsen's
arm. Olsen pushed against the bottom and went
up, using his free arm. The monster trailed
behind, not letting go of his other arm. On
surfacing Olsen clung to the gunwale with
his free hand, hooked it with his leg, clambered into the boat and, with one strong push,
sent the half-man, half-frog, splashing into the
water. The Indians in the boat had jumped
into the water and were swimming shorewards
for all they were worth.

Ichthyander swam back to the boat.

"Listen, Olsen," he said in Spanish, "I must
speak to you about Gutiérrez."

Fantastic as it all seemed at the moment

Olsen had enough good judgement to realize that it was a human being and not a monster he was dealing with.

"Well, I'm listening," he said.

Ichthyander scrambled into the boat, sat down cross-legged in the bows and crossed his paws on his chest.

Why, it's goggles he's got on, Olsen thought, after a good look at the stranger's face.

"My name's Ichthyander. I got a necklace for you from the sea-bottom once."

"But then you had a man's eyes and hands."

Ichthyander smiled and shook his frog-like paws.

"Gloves," he said briefly.

"That's what I thought."

From the shelter of some rocks on the shore the curious Indians watched them speak, though no words carried across to them.

"Do you love Gutiérrez?" Ichthyander asked after a short pause.

"Yes," Olsen said simply.

Ichthyander heaved a deep sigh.

"Does she love you?"

"She loves me too."

"But doesn't she love me?"

"That's her business," Olsen shrugged his shoulders.

"How do you mean? Why, she's your bride."

Though Olsen looked surprised he still retained his calm.

"No, she's not."

"You're lying!" Ichthyander flared up. "I myself heard a swarthy man on horseback call her a bride."

"*My* bride?"

Ichthyander was confused. No, the swarthy man had not said that Gutiérrez was Olsen's bride. But surely a young girl like Gutiérrez could not be the bride of that dark-faced ugly old man? Surely that could not be so? The swarthy man must be her relative. Ichthyander decided to try another tack.

"What were you doing here? Pearl-diving?"

"I must confess I don't like your questions," Olsen said morosely. "Had I not known a little about you from Gutiérrez I should've pushed you off the boat and that's that. And keep your hand from your knife. I can smash your head with an oar before you so much as raise your hand. But I don't see why I shouldn't tell you that I was indeed looking for a pearl."

"The big pearl that I threw into the sea? Gutiérrez told you about it?"

Olsen nodded.

Ichthyander exulted.

"There you are. Why, I told her you wouldn't refuse it. I said she should take it and give it to you. She refused point-blank and now you're looking for it."

"Yes, because now it belongs to the ocean, not you. If I find it I'll owe it only to myself."

"Do you love pearls that much?"

"I'm no woman to love trinkets," retorted Olsen.

"But you can—what's the word now—yes, sell it, get lots of money for it."

Olsen nodded again.

"So you love money?"

"What are you trying to get at?" Olsen asked, somewhat annoyed.

"I must know what Gutiérrez made you a present of her pearls for. You were going to marry her, weren't you?"

"No, I wasn't," said Olsen. "Even if I was it's too late anyway. She is already married."

The blood drained from Ichthyander's face.

"Surely not to that swarthy one," was all he could say.

"Yes. She has married Pedro Zurita."

"But she ... I thought she loved me," Ichthyander said softly.

Olsen was looking at him sympathetically as he lighted up his short pipe.

"Yes, I think she loved you. But you jumped

into the sea before her very eyes and drowned, or at least that was what she thought."

Ichthyander looked up at Olsen in amazement. It was true he had never told Gutiérrez he could live underwater. But it had never entered his head that she could take his leap for suicide.

"I saw her last night," went on Olsen. "Your death has upset her terribly. She was to blame for it, she said."

"But why did she have to marry another one so soon? She—I saved her life. Yes, I did! For a long time I thought she looked like the girl I had pulled out of the sea once. I brought her ashore and hid myself behind some rocks. Then that dark-skinned fellow came—I knew him at the first glance—and tried to convince her it was he who had saved her life."

"Gutiérrez spoke to me about it," Olsen said. "She couldn't quite make her mind up who it was had saved her—Zurita or a strange creature that she had seen for a fleeting moment when coming to. Why didn't you tell her it was you?"

"It's embarrassing to speak about oneself. Besides I wasn't sure at first, in fact until I saw Zurita. But how could she agree?" Ichthyander asked.

"That I don't know myself," Olsen said slowly.

"Please tell me all you know, will you?"

"I work at a button factory, as a shell examiner. That's where I got to know Gutiérrez. She used to bring shells—her father sent her when he was busy. We got friendly. Sometimes we met in the port and went for walks along the shore. Then she told me about her ill luck: a rich Spaniard wooing her."

"The same one? Zurita?"

"That's right, Zurita. Gutiérrez's father—the Indian Baltasar—was all in favour and was doing his best to talk her into marrying him, the princely suitor."

"What's so princely about him? Why, he's so old, ugly, foul-smelling. . . ." Ichthyander could not contain himself.

"For Baltasar, Zurita was about the best son-in-law he could wish for. All the more so because Baltasar was head and ears in Zurita's debt. Zurita could ruin him just like that, if Gutiérrez did not see reason. Just imagine what it was like for her: Zurita's advances on the one hand, her father's nagging on the other. . . ."

"Why didn't Gutiérrez send him packing?

Why didn't you give him a hiding, you, so big and strong?"

Olsen smiled at this outburst but it left him wondering. Ichthyander was not a fool yet his questions were strange somehow. Where had he been brought up?

"That's more easily said than done," Olsen replied. "Zurita and Baltasar would have had the law and the police and the courts on their side. In short, I couldn't."

But that didn't explain things for Ichthyander.

"Well then, why didn't she run away?" he asked.

"That would have been easier, of course. Indeed that was what she wanted to do and I promised her my help. As a matter of fact I'd meant to go up to North America for quite some time, so I told her she could join me and welcome."

"Did you intend to marry her?" Ichthyander asked.

"A queer chap you are," Olsen said and smiled again. "Didn't I tell you we were just friends. What could've happened afterwards I don't know."

"Why didn't you go then?"

"Because we hadn't the money for the fare."

"Is a passage by the *Horrocks* really so expensive?"

"The *Horrocks* my foot. The liner's for the millionaires. Why, man, are you straight from the moon or what?"

Ichthyander flushed in embarrassment and thought he would try and ask no more questions that could show Olsen his ignorance.

"We didn't have enough money for a freight boat, let alone the *Horrocks*. And we had to have a little above that to tide us over the first days on arrival. Jobs are not to be got for the asking up there any more than here."

Ichthyander had another question coming, but he desisted.

"It was then that Gutiérrez decided to sell her pearl necklace."

"If only I had known!" Ichthyander exclaimed, remembering about the pearls he had stored underwater.

"What about?"

"Never mind. Please go on, Olsen."

"Everything was ready for the flight—"

"Wait a minute. And me . . . I mean, how could that be? Does that mean she wanted to leave me too?"

"All this began before you turned up. But then, as far as I know, she meant to let you into it. Perhaps even to invite you to go away with her. Finally she could have written to you later, if she wasn't able to speak to you before she went away."

"But why with you, not with me? It's always you, speaking to you, going away with you...."

"She had known me for over a year, whereas you...."

"Please go on, don't mind me."

"Well, as I said, everything was ready," Olsen went on. "But then you went and jumped into the sea before her very eyes in Zurita's presence. Early next morning I dropped in to see Gutiérrez before my shift. It wasn't my first visit. Baltasar didn't seem to mind. Maybe because he respected the size of my fists, maybe because I looked a good stand-in, in case Zurita cooled off. At any rate Baltasar made no trouble and only begged us to keep well apart in Zurita's presence. Of course the old Indian had no inkling of our plan. That morning I was there to tell Gutiérrez that I had got two fares and that she was to be ready to leave by ten that night. Baltasar met me, in a state of agitation."

" 'Gutiérrez's not in. She's away—for good,' he told me. 'Half an hour ago Zurita drove up in a brand-new gleaming car. Fancy that!' he went on. 'A car's something we never

156

see in our street, specially pulled up slap in front of your own door. Gutiérrez and I ran out. Zurita was already out of the car, inviting Gutiérrez for a ride to the market and back. He knows that's the time she goes there. Gutiérrez looked at the flashy thing. You can understand, I s'ppose, what an attraction it is for a young girl. But Gutiérrez's as sly and distrustful as they make 'em. She says no politely. Never seen anybody so stubborn as that girl!' he exclaimed in anger, but then began laughing. 'Zurita was smart though. You're being shy, he says, let me help you. And he grabbed her and pulled her in and she had only time to shout Father once and they were off.'

" 'I don't think they'll ever come back. Zurita's taken her home, if you ask me,' Baltasar finished his story and I could easily see that he had enjoyed telling it.

" 'Your daughter's been taken away by force under your very eyes and you stand there and tell me it all like a huge joke!' I told Baltasar with indignation.

" 'Why should I worry?' Baltasar looked surprised. 'Had it been anybody else, yes. But Zurita—I've known him for ages. If a skinflint like him could cough up enough money to buy a car, why, he's dead set on Gutiérrez and no mistake. He'll marry her as sure as eggs is eggs. That'll teach her to be stubborn. Should know a good chance when she sees it. There's nothing for her to weep about. Zurita owns a *hacienda*, called 'Dolores,' just outside the town of Paraná. His mother lives up there. Ten to one it's there he's taken my Gutiérrez to.' "

"And you didn't give Baltasar a thrashing?" asked Ichthyander.

"To hear you I should do nothing else but go about beating people up," said Olsen. "I did have a mind to give him a good drubbing though. But then I thought better of it. I thought things could be remedied yet. I won't go into all details. Anyhow as I told you, I managed to see Gutiérrez."

"At the *Hacienda Dolores?*"

"Yes."

"And you didn't kill Zurita and set Gutiérrez free?"

"Now I should be murdering people as well. Who'd think you were so bloodthirsty?"

"I'm not," Ichthyander exclaimed, tears welling up in his eyes. "But this is enough to make one's blood boil!"

Olsen was sorry for Ichthyander.

"You're right," said Olsen. "Zurita and Baltasar are a pair of rascals. They do deserve a thorough beating. But life's more complicated than you apparently think it is. You see, Gutiérrez refused to run away from Zurita."

"What? Refused?" Ichthyander could not believe his ears.

"Yes."

"But why?"

"For one thing, she's convinced that you took your own life because of her. She's taken your death very hard. She must have loved you, poor thing. 'My life's over now, Olsen,' she told me. 'There's nothing I want now. I don't care for anything. I was in a haze when the priest Zurita had invited was performing the wedding ceremony. Nothing is done without God's will, he said putting the wedding ring on my finger. And what God hath joined together, let no man put asunder. I'll be unhappy with Zurita but I'm afraid of drawing God's wrath down on me. I won't leave him.' "

"What nonsense! God indeed! Father says God is old wives' tales!" Ichthyander said hotly. "Surely you could have talked her out of it?"

"Unfortunately it's an old wives' tale that Gutiérrez believes. The missionaries made a devout Catholic of her; I tried my best to show it up for what it was and couldn't. She even said she'd never see me again if I went on abusing God and the Holy Catholic Church in her presence. So I had to ease down. And at the *hacienda* I had no time to go deeper into it anyway. Just enough to exchange a few words. But, there's something else she told me. When the wedding was over, Zurita said with a guffaw, 'Well, one thing's taken care of. The little bird's caught and locked up, now's the turn for the little fish.' He then explained to Gutiérrez, and she to me, what little fish he meant. He said he was going to Buenos Aires to catch the 'sea-devil,' and make Gutiérrez a millionaire's wife. You are not that 'sea-devil' by any chance, are you? You stay underwater for hours, you scare pearl-divers. . . ."

Caution prevented Ichthyander from letting Olsen into his secret. Not that he could have explained it anyway. So leaving Olsen's question unanswered he himself asked:

"What does he want him for?"

"Pedro intends to make the 'sea-devil' pearl-dive for him. If you are that 'sea-devil,' take care!"

"Thanks for the warning," said the amphibian.

Now Ichthyander had not the slightest idea

that on and off he had been headline news in Buenos Aires.

"I can't. . . ." Ichthyander said passionately. "I must see her. Even if it's the last time. The town of Paraná you said? Yes, I know it. It's up the River Paraná. But how do I find the *Hacienda Dolores*?"

Olsen explained.

Ichthyander gave Olsen's hand a firm shake.

"I must apologize. I came to see an enemy and found a friend. Good-bye. I'm off to see Gutiérrez."

"Straightaway?" Olsen was smiling.

"Yes, not losing a minute," Ichthyander replied, jumping overboard and swimming shorewards.

Olsen only shook his head.

PART II

I chthyander's preparations for the journey did not take long. He collected his town suit and shoes, strapped them to his body with the leather belt he carried his knife on, put on his goggles and gloves and set out.

In the Rio de la Plata numerous anchored craft lay in his path, pigmy steam tugs darting in and out. From below the tugs looked like so many water-bugs scuttling here and there. Round him a thin-trunked submarine forest of anchor chains and buoy-ropes strained up to the oil-filmed surface from a floor that was copiously littered with heaps of spilt coal and dumped slag, lengths of worn hose, pieces of sail, discarded tins, bricks, broken bottles, and–closer inshore–dead dogs and cats.

The sun was still up, but down here a grey-brown twilight reigned unchallenged. The River Paraná discharged its waters into the gulf, heavily laden with sediment.

Ichthyander could easily have lost his way in the thicket of chains and ropes but for the guiding current of the inflowing river. It's amazing how untidy people are, he thought, running a fastidious eye over the sea-floor, which looked like one huge rubbish-dump. As he swam towards the head of the gulf, just under the ships' keels, breathing became gradually harder, as for a man in a sealed-up room.

On his way he saw a few corpses. One of them, which he passed quite close, had a smashed head and a length of rope weighted with a stone round the neck. Somebody's crime was buried here. Ichthyander put on speed, wishing to leave the gruesome sight well behind.

But the higher up the gulf he penetrated the

stronger was the oncoming current. There were currents in the ocean too, but he knew how to put them to use, much as the sailor puts to use a fair wind. Here there was only one current, and that was in the wrong direction. It couldn't hold back an excellent swimmer like Ichthyander but it slowed down his progress enough to irritate him.

Suddenly something heavy hurtled down past him, almost brushing his side. A ship's anchor had been dropped. Oho, thought Ichthyander, this seems a dangerous place to swim in, and he looked round him. A big steamer was coming up from behind.

Ichthyander went lower and when the ship's hull was passing above him he clutched at her keel. Colonies of barnacles had formed a rough layer on the steel plates, just allowing him to get a grip. Suspended from the ship's keel in a way not exactly comfortable, he was at least out of danger, and being carried upstream at a reasonable speed.

The ship was now going up the river itself. Ichthyander breathed heavily in the water thick with silt. His arms were getting quite numb but he was loth to part with the ship. What a pity I couldn't take Leading along, he thought, remembering the dolphin. He had been obliged to discard his original plan:

Leading could not have made the whole trip underwater, while Ichthyander would have been afraid to surface in a heavily navigated river.

Ichthyander was finding it increasingly hard to keep his hold, his arms were so numb. Besides he suffered pangs of hunger; he had had nothing to eat for hours. Deciding he should make a break he released his grip and sank onto the river-bed.

In the deepening twilight Ichthyander examined the silty bottom. But he could find neither flounder nor oyster shells. What fish darted about near him were of fresh-water species that he did not know. After several unsuccessful attempts to catch one he decided they were much more cunning than their sea-water kin. Only when night descended and the fish went to sleep did Ichthyander manage to catch a big pike. Its flesh was tough and tasted of silt but the famished amphibian ate with relish, swallowing it bones and all.

Then he thought he would rest a bit. The one advantage of being in a river was that he could at least snatch a few hours of quiet sleep, with no thought of prying sharks or octopuses. He only had to make sure the current did not drag him downstream in his sleep. Ichthyander piled up a few big stones into a rough groyne and settled down in the lee of it, his arm anchored round one of the stones.

However his sleep was short. He felt the approach of a vessel, opened his eyes and saw the signal lights. The vessel was coming upstream. The amphibian quickly went up and prepared to cling on. But this time it was a motor boat with a bottom as smooth as glass, so after a few attempts which nearly carried him against the screw, Ichthyander gave up.

And it wasn't until a few boats had gone downstream that he at last managed to cling fast to a steamship going upriver.

In this way Ichthyander reached the town of Paraná. The first lap of his journey was over. But the most difficult part of it—overland—was still ahead.

Early the next morning Ichthyander swam away from the noisy harbour, found a stretch of river-bank with no sign of life in sight and scrambled ashore. He buried his goggles and gloves on the beach, then dried his suit in the sun and put it on. The crumpled suit made him look like a tramp. But that didn't bother him.

Setting out along the right bank, as told by Olsen, Ichthyander kept asking the fishermen he met the way to the *Hacienda Dolores* owned by Pedro Zurita.

The fishermen eyed him suspiciously and shook their heads.

Hour after hour went by, the heat mounted but he was as uncertain of his way as when he had set out in the morning. On land Ichthyander had no way of finding his bearings in unknown surroundings. Besides his head swam with the heat and he was finding it more and more difficult to concentrate.

From time to time he took a dip in the river to refresh himself.

Finally, when it wanted only a few minutes to four in the afternoon, he happened upon an old peasant, a farm-labourer by his looks. After listening to Ichthyander he nodded.

"Go straight along that road, between the fields," he told him. "When you reach a big pond, cross the bridge, top a little hill and there you are—there'll be your *Doña* Dolores *la Mostacha* for you."

"Why *mostacha*? Dolores is a *hacienda*, isn't it?"

"That's right. But the old mistress of the *hacienda* is also called Dolores. Pedro's her son. A fat old woman with a big moustache. But don't you think of hiring yourself out to her. She'll eat you raw, suit and all. A regular virago, she is. Zurita's brought home a young wife, they say. Her mother-in-law'll make it hard for her," the garrulous old man said.

That must be Gutiérrez, thought Ichthyander.

"Is it far?" he asked.

"You'll get there by the fall of evening," the old man said, having consulted the sun.

Thanking him, Ichthyander hurried on along the road past the fields of wheat and maize, past lush pastures with flocks of grazing sheep. The many hours' tramp had begun to tell on his strength. The road stretched ahead in an endless white ribbon.

His lips were parched but look as he would he could not see water anywhere round. He heartily wished he were in sight of that pond at last. He strained to go quicker, his face was drawn and his breathing laboured. Then that pain in his sides began. He was hungry, too. But there was nothing near the road he could dine off. The sheep grazing on a pasture nearby, were guarded by a shepherd and his dogs. Branches of peach and orange trees laden with ripe fruit were just visible above a stone wall. This wasn't the ocean. Here everything was somebody's property, everything was divided, fenced off and guarded. The birds alone were nobody's, flitting and trilling overhead. But try and catch them. And then, was he allowed to catch them? Perhaps they too belonged to somebody? Here on land one could die of hunger and thirst in the middle of orchards, ponds and herds.

A fat man in a white cap and a white tunic with bright buttons, a revolver holster at his belt, his hands clasped behind his back, was coming towards Ichthyander.

"Can you tell me how far it is to the *Hacienda Dolores?*" asked Ichthyander.

The fat man eyed him suspiciously.

"What d'you want there? Where've you come from?"

"Buenos Aires."

The fat man's eyes became alert.

"I must see someone there," Ichthyander added.

"Hold out your hands," said the man.

This request somewhat surprised Ichthyander but, unsuspectingly, he held out his hands.

The fat man quickly produced a pair of handcuffs from his pocket. The next Ichthyander knew they were clicked to round his wrists.

"There," the fat man muttered, and, giving Ichthyander a push, rapped out, "Come along! I'll take you to the *Hacienda Dolores.*"

"But what've you put these things on my hands for?" Ichthyander asked, staring in bewilderment at the handcuffs.

"None of your lip. Move on!" snapped the man in the tunic.

Ichthyander hung his head and shuffled on. Well, at least he hadn't been turned back, but he had no idea what was going to befall him. He did not know that the previous night a farm nearby had been burgled and a man murdered and that the police were looking for the criminals. Nor did he realize that in his crumpled suit he looked very suspicious. His vague answers clinched the case against him.

The policeman was taking Ichthyander to the nearest village to have him transported to the town of Paraná.

One thing Ichthyander did realize: he was no longer free to go on with his journey. And he resolved to make a bid for freedom at the first chance that presented.

Hugely pleased with his good luck the fat policeman lighted up a long cigar and walking closely behind Ichthyander, started puffing out cloud after cloud of acrid smoke. Ichthyander was suffering torture.

"Would you mind not smoking, please, I find it difficult to breathe," turning, he said to his escort.

"What? Stop smoking? That's a good one!"
The policeman guffawed, his whole face
gathering up in wrinkles. "Delicate, are you?"
and, puffing out a cloud of smoke straight
into Ichthyander's face, he barked, "On with
you!"

The amphibian did as he was told.

At last the pond with its narrow bridge came
into view and Ichthyander involuntarily
quickened pace.

"Not so fast, you'll see your Dolores soon
enough," the fat man cried.

They stepped onto the bridge. When they
were halfway across Ichthyander suddenly
bent over the rail and threw himself into the
water.

That was about the last thing the policeman
could have expected from a man in manacles.

But what the policeman did next was a
complete surprise for Ichthyander too: afraid
his prisoner might drown, in his charge, and
manacled, with all sorts of possible unpleasant
consequences, he jumped in after him. Indeed,
he was so quick in doing this that he managed
to get a grip on Ichthyander's hair and hold
it. Then, risking his scalp, Ichthyander dragged
the policeman bottomwards. Presently his
hair was released. Ichthyander swam to the
side and popped his head above the surface

to see whether the policeman had come up. He had and was treading water, looking round.

"You'll get drowned, damn you! Swim over here!" the policeman yelled, spotting his prisoner's head.

Not a bad idea this, Ichthyander thought, and crying out, "Help! Help!" he sank to the bottom.

From down there he watched the policeman dive for him several times. At last, having lost all hope, the policeman scrambled ashore.

He'll go away now, thought Ichthyander. But the policeman didn't. He seemed to have decided to wait by the corpse for the arrival of the investigating authorities. The fact that the corpse was lying somewhere on the bottom of the pond did not alter anything.

A peasant riding a mule laden with sacks appeared on the road. The policeman ordered the peasant to dump his sacks and take a note to the nearest police station. Things were taking a bad turn for Ichthyander. To top it all there were leeches in the pond. They stuck to his body in swarms and soon he was fighting a losing battle, tearing them desperately off as they came in ever-increasing numbers, yet anxious to limit movement lest a stir in

172

the water should attract the policeman's attention.

In half an hour the peasant was back. He waved his hand in the direction of the road, heaved his sacks and hurried on his way. In still another five minutes a trio of policemen put in an appearance, two of them carrying a light boat on their heads, while the third had the oars and a boat-hook.

The boat was lowered onto the water, two policemen got in and the dragging started. Not that that bothered Ichthyander much at first. It was child's play for him, just keeping moving from one place to another. The dragging round the bridge was thorough but unsuccessful.

The policeman who had arrested Ichthyander was throwing his arms about in a gesture of surprise. That even provided a spot of fun for Ichthyander—but not for long. The policemen had stirred up clouds of silt with their boat-hook. The water thick with it, Ichthyander could not see anything at arm's length and that was dangerous. And what was even worse —he could hardly breathe with all the silt raised.

With his breathing more and more laboured, and the irritation in his gills more and more acute, he felt he could not bear it any longer. He groaned; a few bubbles escaped his mouth. What could he do? He had to come up, there was nothing for it. He had to come up, whatever risk was involved. They would seize him, of course, perhaps beat him up. He didn't care. Ichthyander staggered for the bank and put his head out of the water.

In the boat a policeman gave a hoarse yell, jumped overboard and made flat out for the bank. His companion had dropped down on his belly and was crying, "*Jesús, María y José!*" over and over.

The two policemen on the bank were saying prayers, ashen with fright, trembling, trying to hide one behind the other.

Ichthyander had not expected anything like that and was quite taken aback for a moment. Then he remembered the proverbial superstitiousness of the Spaniard. So the policemen thought he was an apparition from the other world, did they! Well, he would scare them a little more. Baring his teeth and rolling his eyes, he howled horribly and slowly strode up the bank and to the road and away along it, walking at a deliberately measured pace.

None of the policemen made a move to stop him. Their sense of duty had battled with and lost to their superstitious awe.

Dolores—Pedro Zurita's mother—was a stout doughy old woman with a hook-nose, a jutting chin and a thick moustache that added up to produce an odd, almost forbidding effect. The latter adornment, so rare with her sex, had earned her the nickname of *Doña* Dolores *la Mostacha* by which she was known throughout the locality.

When Pedro brought his young bride to her she had greeted the girl with an unceremonious stare. Dolores had an eye only for deficiencies. The girl's beauty struck her, but it was like her not to show it in any way and to decide later, over her pots and pans, that that was just what was wrong with the girl.

"A tasty dish!" she said that day, alone with her son, and shook her head, "Much too tasty!" and, after a sigh, "See you don't run into trouble with a beauty like that for a wife. I wish you'd married a Spanish girl." She paused, then added. "Haughty, too. And her hands, why, she won't do a stroke of work about the house with those soft hands of hers."

"We'll break her to it," Pedro said and bent over his accounts.

Dolores yawned and, leaving Pedro to his

work, went out into the garden, cool with the evening. She was fond of sitting in the moon-lit mimosa-scented garden, all by herself, dreaming.

She went past a border of lilies gleaming white in the moonlight, past whispering laurel bushes, to a bank overgrown with myrtles, let herself down onto it and was soon lost in her dreams. In them she was buying a neighbour out of his farm, building new sheds and out-houses, breeding flocks of fine-fleece sheep.

"Pest on you," the old woman cried angrily, slapping her cheek. "Those mosquitoes won't leave a body in peace for a moment." Clouds had banked the skies and the garden was dark. Against the darker sky a bluish band low on the horizon—the glow of the lights of the town of Paraná—gained in lightness.

Suddenly, above the low stone fence, she spotted a man's head. A pair of manacled hands were lifted into view and the man eased himself carefully over the fence.

The old woman shuddered with terror. An escaped convict in her garden! She wanted to cry out but couldn't, tried to get up and run but her legs buckled under her. From her bank, spell-bound, she watched the stranger.

Meanwhile he had made his way cautiously among the bushes to the house and was stealing from window to window, peering in.

Then she heard him—or was she mistaken?— call softly, "Gutiérrez!"

That's your beauty for you, she thought. That's the type she goes about with. Wouldn't be surprised if she murdered me and Pedro, burgled the place and made away with that convict of hers.

A feeling of gloating hatred for Gutiérrez seized the old woman. Her strength recovered, she jumped up and waddled quickly inside.

"Quick!" Dolores whispered to her son. "There's a convict in our garden. He's calling for Gutiérrez."

Pedro rushed out as though the house were on fire, seized a spade lying by the garden path and ran round the corner.

Standing at the wall and peering into a window was a stranger in a crumpled suit, his hands manacled.

"Damn you!" Zurita muttered and brought his spade down on the crown of the man's head.

The man fell as though cut down.

"That's done for him," Zurita said in a low voice.

"It has indeed," Dolores, who had caught up

with him, agreed in a tone she would have used if her son had squashed a scorpion.

Zurita looked at his mother.

"Where shall we take him to?"

"The pond," the old woman indicated. "It's deep."

"He'll come to the surface."

"We'll weight him. Hold on a second."

Dolores ran inside and searched feverishly for a sack to put the dead man in. But she had sent all her sacks to the mill with wheat that morning. So she took a pillow-case and a length of string.

"There're no sacks," she told her son. "Here, put some stones in the pillow-case and tie it up to his handcuffs."

Zurita nodded, heaved the body on his back and dragged it to a small pond in the back of the garden.

"Mind the blood," Dolores whispered to him, waddling behind, pillow-case and string in hand.

"You wash it away," Pedro replied, putting the man's head down, however, so that the blood would spill on the ground.

At the pond Zurita quickly stuffed the pillow-case with stones, tied it securely to the young man's hands and shoved the body into the water.

"I must change." Pedro glanced up at the sky. "It's going to rain. By the morning there won't be a trace of blood on the grass."

"What about the pond, won't the water turn red?" asked Dolores.

"No, not in a running-water pond."

"Oh, to hell with it!" growled Zurita and shook his fist in the direction of the house.

"There's your beauty for you," the old woman was saying in a whining voice as she followed her son towards the house.

* * *

Gutiérrez had been given a room in the attic. That night she could not go to sleep what with the stuffiness, stinging mosquitoes and the cheerless thoughts that crowded her mind.

The memory of Ichthyander still came between her and her sleep. Her husband she did not love. Her mother-in-law she detested, yet here she was sharing their roof with them.

Gutiérrez thought she heard Ichthyander's voice calling her. A noise like muffled voices floated up to her window. She listened but heard nothing. Towards dawn she decided that she was not to fall asleep that night at all. She went out into the garden.

The sun was not up yet. The garden lay in front of her, wrapped in pre-dawn haze. The clouds had been chased away and heavy drops of dew sparkled in the grass and on the trees. In her light gown, barefoot, Gutiérrez was walking over the grass. Suddenly she stopped short. In the walk, outside her window, the sand was blood-stained. A blood-stained spade was lying nearby.

A crime had been committed that night. Or was there some other explanation for these blood stains?

Involuntarily Gutiérrez followed the track which led her to the pond.

Suppose the key to the crime is hidden in the pond, she thought, peering, scared, into the greenish water.

Down there, in that murky water, looking straight at her was Ichthyander's face. There was a wound near the temple. The face expressed suffering mingled with happiness.

Could she have gone mad?

Gutiérrez wanted to run away, but she couldn't. Nor could she tear her eyes away from Ichthyander's face.

Meanwhile Ichthyander's face was slowly coming up, till, with a soft ripple, it was clear of the water. Ichthyander stretched his manacled hands towards Gutiérrez and smiled wanly.

"Gutiérrez!" he said, "My dearest! At last—" but he did not finish.

Clutching at her head Gutiérrez was crying:

"Be gone! Be gone, unlucky ghost! I know you're dead. Why should you appear to me?"

"No, no, Gutiérrez, I'm not dead," the ghost hastened to reply, "I didn't drown. Forgive me. . . . There are things you don't know about me. . . . Why didn't I tell you. . . . Oh, don't go away, listen to me. I'm alive, here, touch my hands. . . ."

He was stretching his hands towards her. She kept staring at him.

"Don't be afraid, I'm alive. . . . I can live underwater. I'm not like other people. I can live underwater. I didn't drown that time I jumped into the sea. I did it because it was difficult for me to breathe on land."

Ichthyander swayed; then went on, as hastily and as disjointedly as before:

"I've been looking for you, Gutiérrez. Last night your husband struck me on the head when I was standing outside your window and then threw me into the pond. In the water I came to. I managed to get that stone-weighted sack off but I couldn't," here Ichthyander showed up the handcuffs, "these...."

Gutiérrez was almost convinced now.

"But why are your hands manacled?"

"I'll tell you about it later. Come away with me, Gutiérrez. We'll hide at my father's, nobody can find us there.... And we'll be together.... Feel my hands, Gutiérrez. Olsen told me people call me the 'sea-devil' but I'm human. Why are you afraid of me?"

Covered with silt from head to foot Ichthyander waded out of the pond and sank wearily onto the grass.

Gutiérrez bent over him and took him by the hand.

"My poor boy," she said.

"What a pleasant rendezvous!" a mocking voice suddenly came to them.

They looked round and saw Zurita standing nearby.

Zurita, like Gutiérrez, had not been able to sleep a wink that night. He had come into the garden, attracted by Gutiérrez's cry, and had heard all that had followed. When Pedro realized that the "sea-devil" he had been so long trying to catch was at arm's length from him he thanked his lucky stars and decided to take Ichthyander to the *Jellyfish* there and then. But then he had second thoughts.

"I don't think you'll be able to carry Gutiérrez to Doctor Salvator. She's my wife, you know. Besides you're wanted by the police."

"But I've done nothing wrong!" the young man cried.

"People who've done nothing wrong are not issued with nice little bracelets like those. And as you're now in my hands I feel it's only my duty to hand you over to the police."

"Surely you are not going to do that?" Gutiérrez asked her husband indignantly.

"My duty points that way," Pedro said, shrugging his shoulders.

"Nice thing that'd be," cut in Dolores, who had just appeared on the scene, "letting loose a convict. And what for? For prying in another man's garden and looking for a chance to carry away his wife?"

Gutiérrez went across to her husband, took hold of his hands and said gently:

"Let him go. Please. I've done you no wrong. . . ."

Dolores shook her head vigorously, afraid her son would give in.

"Don't listen to her, Pedro!" she shouted.

"I can't resist a woman's entreaty," Zurita said urbanely. "I'll do as you wish."

"Hardly married and already tied to her apron-strings," the old woman said grumpily.

"Wait a minute, Mother. We'll file your handcuffs, my young fellow, rig you up in something decent and take you on board the *Jellyfish*. When we're in the Rio de la Plata you can jump overboard wherever you please. But I will only let you go on one condition: you must forget Gutiérrez. And Gutiérrez, I'll take you along, as well. You'll be safer with me."

"You're better than I thought you were," Gutiérrez said sincerely.

Zurita gave a complacent twirl to his moustache and bowed to his wife.

Dolores knew her son well enough to guess that he was planning something nasty. But, to play his game, she went on grumbling, "Tied to her apron-strings that's what you are. Well, you deserve all you'll get."

FULL SPEED AHEAD!

"Salvator's coming tomorrow. My fever's kept me away just when there was a lot for us to talk about," Cristo was saying to Baltasar in his shop. "Cock your ears, brother, and don't interrupt me, so's I won't forget anything."

Still weak after the fever Cristo paused, marshalling his thoughts, then continued:

"We've done a hell of a lot for Zurita,

brother. He's more brass than both of us but he's out to get still more. He wants to catch the 'sea-devil'—"

Baltasar made to speak.

"Hold it, brother, else I forget something. Zurita wants the 'sea-devil' to slave for him. And d'you know what that 'sea-devil' is? A regular treasure. Untold riches. The 'sea-devil' can pick pearls from the sea-bottom—any amount of 'em. But that's not all. On the sea-bottom there's plenty of sunken treasure. He can get it for us. I say 'us,' not Zurita, and I mean it. D'you know, brother, that Ichthyander's in love with Gutiérrez?"

Baltasar wanted to say something but Cristo didn't let him.

"Keep quiet and listen, will you. I can't speak when people interrupt me. Yes, Ichthyander's in love with Gutiérrez. There isn't much gets past me. When I twigged that I told myself, 'Not a bad thing that,' I said. Let him fall in love with her good and proper. He'll make a better husband—and son-in-law—than Zurita. And Gutiérrez too loves Ichthyander. I've shadowed them, not interfering with Ichthyander in any way. Let them meet as often as they wish, I thought."

Baltasar sighed but did not try to say anything.

"And that's not all, brother. Listen further. I'd like to recall to your memory things that happened many, many years ago. About twenty years back it was, you'll remember, I was accompanying your wife home from a visit to her people. We'd been to the mountains to bury her mother. On the way your wife died, giving birth to a dead child. At that time I didn't tell you everything. Wanted to spare your feelings. Here's the whole story. Your wife did die on the way here, that's true, but the child was born alive, though very weak. It was in a small Indian village it all happened. And an old woman told me that a great miracle-worker, God Salvator, lived not far away. . . ."

Baltasar became all ears.

"She advised me to carry the child to Salvator, saying he'd cure it. I did as she told. Salvator took the boy—for a boy it was—shook his head and said, 'It's very difficult to save him.' But still he took him in. I waited there till nightfall. When it grew dark a Negro came out and told me the child was dead. Then I went away. . . .

"So," Cristo went on, after a pause, "Salvator told me through the Negro that the child was dead. Now I had noticed a birthmark on the newly-born. Somehow I remembered it, shape and all."

There was another pause, then Cristo took up his story again.

"Not long ago Ichthyander came home, wounded in the neck. When I was bandaging him, I lifted the collar of his mail and saw a birthmark, exactly like your son's."

Opening eyes wide with excitement Baltasar asked:

"You think Ichthyander's my son?"

"Keep quiet, brother, and listen. Yes, that's exactly what I do think. Salvator lied to me. Your son did not die, Salvator made a 'sea-devil' out of him."

"Oh!" Baltasar cried, beside himself. "How dare he do it! I'll kill him with my own hands!"

"Keep quiet. Salvator's stronger'n you. And then I might've made a mistake. It's twenty years. Somebody else might have a birthmark exactly on the same spot. Ichthyander might be your son and again he might not. You must play your hand careful like. You go to Salvator and tell him that Ichthyander's your son. I'll be your witness. You will demand your son be returned to you. Failing that you will say you will sue him for maiming children. That'll give him a proper scare. If he's obstinate you will go to court. If we can't pull it off in the courts Ichthyander'll just marry Gutiérrez and that's that. After all she's only your adopted daughter. . . ."

Baltasar had jumped up from his stool and started pacing up and down the shop, all but treading on the crabs and shells on the floor.

"My son! My son! Oh, what a misfortune!"

"Why a misfortune?" asked Cristo, surprised.

"I've listened to you, now you listen to me. While you were laid up with your fever Gutiérrez was married to Pedro Zurita."

The news made Cristo stagger.

"And Ichthyander, my poor son," Baltasar said, hanging his head, "is in Zurita's hands."

"Impossible," said Cristo.

"Yes. Ichthyander's on board the *Jellyfish*. This morning Zurita was here to see me. He laughed and swore at us. He said we'd been cheating him. Just think, he caught Ichthyander all on his own, without any help from us. He won't pay us anything. But I wouldn't have taken anything from him anyway. I'm not selling my own son."

Baltasar, distraught, dashed about the shop. Cristo eyed him disapprovingly. It was a case of all hands to the pump. But Baltasar could sooner ruin things, taking on like that. Himself, Cristo did not believe much in Baltasar's fatherhood. True he had seen that birthmark on the newly-born. But was that enough to build a whole case on? Seeing a similar birthmark on Ichthyander's neck he had decided to cash in on it. How could he have known Baltasar would carry on like a madman. And then the news he had learned from Baltasar had given him quite a scare.

"No time for tears now. We've got to act. Salvator's coming tomorrow at dawn. Brace up and listen. You will wait for me at dawn on the breakwater. We've got to save Ichthyander. But, mind now, don't go and tell Salvator you're Ichthyander's father. Where's Zurita bound for?"

"He didn't say but I think it's north. He made up his mind long ago to go up to the coast of Panama."

Cristo nodded.

"So remember, you're to be up and on the breakwater by first light. And stick around there even if you have to wait till nightfall."

Cristo hurried home. All that night he thought of the meeting with Salvator. There was no way out. He had to face it and have a good story ready. Salvator arrived at dawn. As he was greeting his master, Cristo's face wore an expression of distressed loyalty.

"We've had a misfortune," he said, "I warned Ichthyander not to swim out into the gulf. . . ."

"What's happened to him?" Salvator asked impatiently.

"He was captured and taken on board a schooner. I—"

Salvator had gripped Cristo's shoulders and was peering closely into his eyes. Short as it lasted, Cristo could not help changing colour under that searching glance. Then Salvator knitted his brows, muttered something and unclenched his hands.

"You will tell me about it in detail later."

Then he called a Negro, said a few words to him in a language Cristo did not know and again turned to the Indian.

"Follow me!" Salvator ordered.

Without resting from the journey or even changing his travelling clothes, Salvator strode out of the house and across the garden. Cristo could hardly keep up with him. At the third wall two Negroes caught up with them.

"I watched over Ichthyander day and night, like a dog," Cristo was saying, panting. "I never left his side. . . ." But Salvator would not listen to him. Standing at the pool he was tapping his foot impatiently as he watched the water gush out through the yawning hatches.

"Follow me," Salvator ordered again and hurried down the steps that led underground. Cristo and the two Negroes followed the doctor into the darkness. Salvator ran down the steps, taking two at a time, apparently quite at home in the maze of subterranean passages.

On the bottom landing Salvator did not turn on the light as once before but, after a moment's feeling about with his hand, opened a door to his right and strode on along a dark corridor. There were no steps there and, despite complete darkness, Salvator was going very quick now.

I hope to God there are no man-traps here, Cristo was thinking, hurrying after Salvator. They had been going quite a long time when Cristo felt the floor begin to slope down gently. He thought he could hear a faint splash of water. Then their journey was over. Salvator who was well ahead of them had stopped and switched on the light. Cristo found himself in a large cave, standing on a piece of stone flooring set into the big oblong of water that converged with the sloping ceiling at the far end. On the water, at the edge of the flooring Cristo saw a midget submarine. The little party went on board the boat. Salvator switched on the light in the cabin, while one Negro was battening down the upper hatch and the other revving the engine. Cristo felt the boat shudder, slowly turn round, submerge and as slowly move forward. After two minutes or so they surfaced. Salvator and Cristo came out on deck. Cristo had never been on board a submarine before and looked round with interest.

"Where are Ichthyander's captors heading?"

"Up north, along the coast," said Cristo. "I hope you will forgive my boldness, master, if I suggest you take my brother along. He's been warned and is waiting on the shore."

"Whatever for?"

"Ichthyander was captured by the pearl trader Zurita—"

"How do you know all this?" Salvator took him up short.

"I described the schooner to my brother and he was sure it was Pedro Zurita's *Jellyfish*. My guess is Zurita wants to use Ichthyander for pearl-diving. And Baltasar—that's my brother—knows all there is to know about the pearling grounds round here. You'll find him useful."

Salvator pondered.

"Good. We'll take your brother along."

The boat veered shorewards where Baltasar could already be seen waiting to be picked up. From the breakwater Baltasar looked, frowningly, at the man who had stolen and mutilated his son. However, when the submarine came nearer inshore, he bowed politely to Salvator, before wading aboard.

"Full speed ahead!" ordered Salvator.

He stayed on deck, planted firmly, peering into the wide ocean.

THE EXTRAORDINARY PRISONER

Zurita removed Ichthyander's manacles as he had promised, gave him some clothes and took him to the river where he even let him collect his gloves and goggles. But as soon as they were on board the *Jellyfish* Ichthyander was seized by the crew, acting on Zurita's orders, and locked in the hold. At Buenos Aires Zurita made a short stop to take on stores. He went to see Baltasar to show off his luck and then pulled out of harbour and hugged the coast, making for Rio de Janeiro. He intended to run north the length of South America and only start pearl-diving in the Caribbean Sea.

Gutiérrez he had accommodated in the captain's cabin. He had assured her that he had let Ichthyander go in the Rio de la Plata. However she soon knew it wasn't true. In the evening Gutiérrez heard faint cries and recognized Ichthyander's voice. She was alone in the cabin and when she tried to go out she found the door locked. She drummed with her fists on it and shouted but nobody paid the least attention.

Hearing Ichthyander's cries Zurita let out a string of coarse oaths, left the bridge and, followed by an Indian sailor, went down below into the dark and stuffy hold.

"What the hell are you yelling for?" Zurita asked.

"I'm—I'm suffocating," Ichthyander's voice came up to him. "I can't live without water. It's too stuffy here. Let me swim away. I won't last to see the morning."

Zurita clanged the hatch in place and came on deck.

Suppose he really does croak, he thought worriedly. There's no good in that.

He ordered a barrel to be lowered into the hold and pumped full of water.

"Here's a bath for you," Zurita said to Ichthyander. "You can have your swim. And tomorrow I'll let you swim in the sea."

Ichthyander got into the barrel. The Indian crew pressed round the hatch, in goggle-eyed wonder. They did not know yet that the prisoner was the "sea-devil" in flesh.

"Get the hell out of here!" Zurita shouted at them from the hatchway.

Far from being able to swim Ichthyander could not even stretch full-length in the barrel and had to crouch for a full dip. Besides the barrel had been used for keeping salt pork in and the water in it was soon giving off a foul stench, making things not much better for Ichthyander than they had been before.

Meanwhile the schooner sped north, running before a fresh south-eastener.

Zurita went down to his cabin from the bridge in the bleary pre-dawn hour. He hoped his wife would have been long in bed. But he found her sitting up at the narrow table, her head resting on her arms. On his entry Gutiérrez rose and in the dim light of the lamp hanging from the ceiling he saw a pale determined face.

"You deceived me," she said in a hollow voice.

Somewhat disconcerted, even embarrassed, under his wife's glaring eyes, yet anxious to conceal it, Zurita affected an I'm-sure-I-don't-know-what-you-mean expression and gave his moustache a smart twist.

"Ichthyander chose to stay on board the *Jellyfish* to be near you," he said banteringly.

13* 195

"That's a lie! You're a mean and despicable man. I hate you!" Without warning she snatched a dagger from its place on the wall and swung it at Zurita.

"Oho," said Zurita as he caught her hand and gave it a savage squeeze that made her drop the weapon.

Then he kicked the dagger out of the cabin and let go of his wife's hand.

"That's better," he said. "A drink of iced water should do your nerves a power of good."

And he went out and locked the door.

As he came out on deck the eastern horizon was turning rosy while the still hidden sun had set the flimsy clouds afire. Salty and fresh, the morning breeze filled the sails. Sea-gulls wheeled above, on the look-out for unwary fish.

When the sun had come up Zurita was still pacing the deck, his hands clasped behind his back.

"Well, I've managed worse things, haven't I," he finally said to himself.

Then he ordered the crew to furl the sails. Presently the *Jellyfish* was riding at anchor on the lumpy seas.

"Fetch the prisoner and the chain," Zurita ordered. He'd been itching to test Ichthyander's performance as pearl-diver since he'd brought him on board. Besides he'll perk up a bit in the water, he thought.

Two Indians frogmarched Ichthyander out on deck to the mizzen and stopped there. He threw a glance round him. The ship's rail was only a few paces away. Without warning Ichthyander lunged for the rail and was about to jump overboard when Zurita's heavy fist caught him on the side of his head. He dropped without as much as a groan.

"Haste doesn't pay," Zurita said sententiously.

There was a clang of iron as one of the sailors lugged out on deck a coil of thin chain ending in a band, also made of iron. Zurita adjusted the band round the still unconscious amphibian's middle and locked it.

"Pour some water on his head," he told the sailors.

After a while the young man came to himself and stared, bewildered, at the chain to which he was shackled.

"That's to stop you running away," Zurita explained. "I'm going to let you into the sea. You'll be looking for pearl shells for me. The more pearls you find the longer you stay in the sea. But no funny business, mind, or back you go into your barrel. Understand? Now, is that a bargain?"

Ichthyander nodded.

He was willing to get for Zurita all the treasures of the sea, so long as he could stay in its clean waters.

Zurita, the chained Ichthyander and his Indian escort went to the rail again. Gutiérrez's cabin was on the other side of the ship: Zurita did not particularly wish her to see Ichthyander in irons.

Ichthyander was lowered into the water and onto the sea-bottom. If he could only break the chain! But it was too strong for him and, resignedly, Ichthyander set to collecting pearl shells and putting them into the bag that hung from his side. The iron band pressed his sides, making breathing rather difficult. And yet Ichthyander felt almost happy after having been doubled up for a whole night in that reeky barrel.

Up on deck the sailors, all agog, watched the happenings. Minutes passed but the man on the sea-bed showed no sign of coming up. At first bubbles of air had appeared on the surface but soon even these ceased.

"I'll be eaten up by a shark if he's got a gasp of air left in them lungs of his. Looks he feels hisself as much at home down there as a fish," an old pearl-diver said in amazement, peering into the water below where the young man could be easily seen crawling on all fours along the sea-bed.

"May be it's the 'sea-devil' himself?" a sailor said softly.

"Sea-devil or no sea-devil, the captain's made a jolly good bargain," said the first mate. "A diver like this is worth a dozen."

The sun was close to the zenith when Ichthyander tugged at the chain to be pulled up. His bag was brim-full and he wanted to empty it so that he could go on with his work.

The Indian sailors hauled up the wonder diver in a trice. Everybody was dying to see the catch.

Ordinarily pearl shells are left alone for some days to rot but this time Zurita and his crew were far too impatient. So everybody set to work, prising the shells open with knives.

When they had finished with the shells everybody began to speak at once. A clamour of eager voices broke on deck. Perhaps Ichthyander had been lucky to strike a paying spot, but anyway what he had brought up in his very first bag surpassed everybody's expectations. Among the numerous pearls there were a score of heavies, of excellent shape and exquisite colouring. Indeed his very first catch had brought Zurita a fortune. For the price of one of the bigger pearls he could buy a new schooner. Zurita was on the road to wealth. His dreams were coming true.

Then Zurita became aware of the greedy glances the sailors were throwing at the pearls. He didn't like it and hastened to scoop the pearls into his straw hat.

"It's time we all had breakfast," he said dismissing the crew. "You're not a bad diver, Ichthyander. I've got a spare cabin. I'm going to give it over to you. It won't be so close there. And I'll have a zinc tank made for you, though you may not need it, seeing as you're likely to swim in the sea every day. Chained, to be sure. But what can I do? You'd swim away on me otherwise, back to your crabs."

Ichthyander hated to speak with Zurita. But so long as he was that man's prisoner he should at least try and get decent lodgings out of him.

"A tank's better than a stinky barrel," he said to Zurita, "but you'll have to change water often for me to breathe comfortably."

"How often?"

"Every half hour," said Ichthyander. "Running water'd be still better."

"I can see your head's turned with success. I've praised you a little and here you are, demanding things, picking and choosing."

"I'm not picking and choosing," Ichthyander said in a hurt voice. "I'm—don't you see, if you put a big fish into a pail of water it soon goes to sleep. A fish breathes oxygen out of the water and I—I'm no more than a very big fish really," Ichthyander said with a self-conscious smile.

"I don't know about oxygen but I do know that fish croak if you don't change their water. Perhaps you're right. But pumping water into your tank round the clock will cost me a pretty penny, more than your pearls are worth. You'll ruin me that way."

Now Ichthyander had no clear idea about the prices pearls fetch, neither did he know that Zurita paid his crew next to nothing. He believed what he said.

"If you find it too expensive to keep me, let me swim away!" exclaimed Ichthyander and looked longingly at the ocean.

"Smart, aren't you," Zurita guffawed.

"Please. I will bring you pearls of my own free will. I've collected a heap of smooth round pearls, this high," and Ichthyander touched his knee, "all alike and as big as a bean. I'll give you all of them, to the last one, if you only let me go."

That virtually took Zurita's breath away.

"Can't be true," he managed to say, trying to sound cool.

"I've never lied in my life," Ichthyander flared up.

"Where's that treasure of yours buried?" Zurita asked, no longer able to conceal his excitement.

"In a cave under the sea. Save for Leading nobody knows where it is."

"Who's Leading?"

"My dolphin."

"Oh, is that so?"

What devilry is this? he thought. But if what he says is true—and I've a hunch it is—why, it's bigger than anything I've ever dreamed of. I'll be rich beyond imagination. Rothschilds and Rockefellers will look a bunch of beggars in comparison. I've a feeling the young fellow can be trusted. Shall I risk it?

But Zurita wasn't one to treat any man's word as sufficient security. And then doing Ichthyander out of his treasure and keeping him had a greater appeal for Zurita anyhow. Then his plan flashed on him. If Gutièrrez asks Ichthyander to fetch his pearls he'll do it, he thought.

"Perhaps I will let you go," said Zurita, "but not straightway. I'll keep you for a while. Yes. I've got my reasons, of course. And I fancy you won't have cause to regret a little delay either. And while you're my guest, even if an unwilling one, I will see to it that you're comfortable. Perhaps a big iron cage'd be just the job for you, seeing as a tank'd involve too much expense. You'd be lowered overboard in it–good for keeping the sharks off you too."

"Yes, but I must sometimes breathe air as well."

"Well, we'll have you pulled up for that. That'll be cheaper than pumping water into a tank. In a word, I'll see to everything, you'll be pleased."

Zurita was in excellent spirits. He even ordered a tot of rum to be issued to all hands at breakfast–something that was never done on board his schooner.

While Ichthyander was being taken back into the hold awaiting a tank or cage, Zurita went below and unlocked the captain's cabin. Not sure he was welcome, he halted in the doorway, showing his hatful of pearls to Gutiérrez.

"I keep my promises," he began, beaming at her, "and I know that my wife is fond of pearls–plenty of pearls. But you need a good diver for that. That's why I've kept Ichthyander. Look, this is just one morning's catch."

Gutiérrez affected a casual glance at the

pearls. It was all she could do to suppress an exclamation of surprise. But Zurita sensed it and gave a complacent laugh.

"You'll be the richest woman in Argentina, in the whole of America. You'll have everything money can buy. I'll build a palace for you that will make kings gape with envy. Please accept the first instalment—half of these pearls."

"No. I won't touch a single one of those pearls got at the cost of a crime," Gutiérrez retorted sharply. "And, please, leave me alone."

Zurita was dismayed and annoyed. He had not expected anything like that.

"Wait a minute. There's something I wanted to ask you. Would you like me to let Ichthyander go?"

Gutiérrez looked at Zurita distrustfully as she tried to guess what new ruse he had thought up.

"What next?" she asked him coldly.

"His fate's in your hands. You have only to bid Ichthyander bring on board the *Jellyfish* the pearls he's hiding somewhere under the water and he'll be free to go where he pleases."

"Now listen to me, Zurita. I don't believe a single word of yours. You're out to have the pearls and Ichthyander. I'm as sure of that as of the fact that I'm the wife of the biggest liar and double-crosser that ever walked in shoeleather. Remember this and never try again to make me party to your evil doings. Once more—leave me alone, please."

There didn't seem to be anything more Zurita could say, so he went out. Back in his own cabin he poured the pearls into a pouch, put it carefully into the chest, locked it and went up on deck. What his wife had just said to him did not affect him much. In his mind's eye he saw himself a rich man with people crowding to pay homage to him.

He mounted the bridge and lit a cigar. The dreams of riches to come were warming him pleasantly. Usually alert, he did not see the sailors gather in groups to discuss something.

THE ABANDONED "JELLYFISH"

Zurita was standing near the rail, opposite the foremast, when at a sign from the first mate he was attacked by several sailors at once. They were unarmed but there were many of them. However Zurita did not prove an easy prey. Two sailors clutched him from the rear. He tore himself from the attackers, backed a few steps and threw himself, with all his might, against the rail.

With groans the sailors loosened their grip and slumped down on the deck. Zurita straightened up the moment the others tried to lay hands on him again and let out right and left with his fists. He never went about without his revolver but the attack had been so unexpected that he had had no time to draw it. Backing slowly he approached the foremast and then, with the agility of a monkey, he started climbing up it.

A sailor caught him by his foot but with the heel of his other foot Zurita struck him a blow on his head and the man rolled down on the deck, stunned. Zurita reached the top and settled there, swearing. For a time he felt himself safer. He pulled out his revolver and shouted:

"The first who makes for me will have light let through his head."

Below the sailors were noisily discussing their next move.

"There's guns in the captain's cabin," the first mate tried to outshout the rest. "Let's go and force the door."

Several men made for the hatch.

Looks I'm done for, thought Zurita, they'll pot me like a sitting duck.

He threw a glance at the sea as though look-ing for help. And he could not believe his eyes when he saw a submarine approaching the *Jellyfish* at great speed, bouncing and nose-diving.

Zurita wished fervently she would not submerge. Then he saw people at the conning tower.

"Help! Murder!" Zurita bawled at the top of his voice.

They must have seen him on the submarine. Without reducing her speed she continued heading straight for the *Jellyfish*.

Armed sailors had poured out on deck and were now standing about, uncertain what to do. Surely they couldn't kill Zurita within sight of the sub—naval by her looks too.

However, Zurita's triumph was short-lived. On the submarine's deck he spotted Baltasar and Cristo standing next to a tall man with an aggressive nose and the eyes of an eagle. The latter shouted:

"Pedro Zurita! You will immediately surren-der Ichthyander whom you are keeping pris-oner on board your schooner. I give you five minutes, after which time I'll sink her."

The traitors, Zurita thought as he stared, bitter hatred in his eyes, at Cristo and Balta-sar, the God-damned traitors. But come to it

I'd rather lose Ichthyander than my own head.

"I'll bring him up directly," Zurita shouted, climbing down the shrouds.

His attackers had decided their own safety was in danger. Some of them hastily lowered boats from the davits, others jumped overboard and swam for the shore. It was every man for himself.

Zurita ran down the companion ladder to his cabin, snatched the pouch with pearls out of his chest, thrust it inside his shirt and took along a belt and a bandana. The next moment he unlocked Gutiérrez's cabin, gathered her up into his arms and carried her out on deck.

"Ichthyander's a bit unwell. He's in the boat," Zurita said as he put her into a boat, lowered it on the water and sprang in himself.

The submarine could not give the boat chase for the water was too shallow for her. But Gutiérrez had already recognized Baltasar on her deck.

"Father, save Ichthyander! He's—" but she could not finish, for Zurita gagged her with the bandana and started, hurriedly, tying her arms with the belt.

"Take your hands off the woman!" Salvator ordered.

"This woman's my wife and nobody's a

right to come between us," Zurita shouted back and pulled away.

"Nobody's a right to treat a woman in that way," shouted Salvator. "Ship your oars or I'll shoot."

But Zurita went on rowing hard. Salvator levelled his revolver. The bullet hit the boat above the water-line.

Zurita picked Gutiérrez up as a shield.

"Go on!" he shouted.

Gutiérrez was struggling in his arms.

"A prize scoundrel, he is!" Salvator said and put down his revolver.

Baltasar jumped into the water and swam towards the boat. But Zurita was already far ahead. Another pull and a wave carried the boat ashore. Zurita picked Gutiérrez up and disappeared behind an outcropping of rocks.

Seeing he could not overtake Zurita, Baltasar headed for the schooner and pulled himself aboard by the anchor chain. The next moment he disappeared down below, in search of Ichthyander. After some time he came into view again.

"Ichthyander isn't on board!" Baltasar shouted to Salvator.

"But he's alive and must be somewhere near," said Cristo. "That's at least what Gutiérrez had time to tell us before that brute gagged her. Otherwise we'd know now where to look for him."

Scanning the ocean's surface Cristo saw a ship's mast tops just showing above the water. He thought that Ichthyander could be down in that wreck.

"Perhaps Zurita had sent Ichthyander to look for treasures on board that wreck?" said Cristo.

Baltasar picked up a chain with a band at one end to show them.

"Looks like Zurita was lowering Ichthyander into the water chained to this thing. Without it he would have swum away. No, he can't be on that ship."

"No," Salvator said pensively. "We've licked Zurita but it's a barren victory."

THE SUNKEN SHIP

They had no way of knowing what had happened on board the *Jellyfish* that morning.

All through the night the crew had put their heads together and by the morning a plot had been formed to attack and kill Zurita at the first opportunity and take possession of ship and diver.

Zurita was up and on the bridge with first

light. The wind had let up and the *Jellyfish* slowly proceeded downwind at a couple of knots.

Then Zurita spotted a dim something ahead. Through his binoculars that something turned into the radiomasts of a sunken ship.

Presently Zurita noticed a life-buoy floating on the surface.

He ordered a boat on the water to pick it up.

When it was brought up to Zurita he saw, to his astonishment, the word *Mafalda* block-lettered on it.

"*Mafalda* sunk?" whistled Zurita. He knew that big American express liner. There must be lots of valuable things on a ship like that, he thought. Suppose I send Ichthyander to get them. But will the chain be long enough? Hardly. On the other hand Ichthyander won't come back if let away without it.

Zurita's mind resembled a battle-ground where avarice and caution were struggling for the upper hand.

Slowly the *Jellyfish* was drawing nearer to the masts sticking out of the water.

The crew crowded at the rail. The wind dropped dead. The schooner came to a stand-still.

"I once had my berth on the *Mafalda*," said

one of the sailors. "A good ship she was. Big as a town. Rich Americans used to cruise on her."

The *Mafalda* must have sunk without having radioed her SOS, Zurita was thinking. Perhaps her WT was out of order. Otherwise the place would have been lousy with launches, speedboats, yachts from all the neighbouring ports loaded with officials, reporters, cameramen, salvage crews and what not. He couldn't throw away a chance like that, could he. He'd have to risk letting Ichthyander go without the chain. There was no other way. But how could he make Ichthyander come back? And if he must take a risk, why not take it sending Ichthyander for his ransom, his pile of pearls? But was it really all that valuable? Was Ichthyander not laying it on thick?

Of course he must get both treasures. The pile of pearls would stay where it was. Nobody could find it without Ichthyander's help, and that made it safe as long as Ichthyander was in his hands. As to the treasures on board the *Mafalda*, they would be beyond his reach in a matter of days, perhaps even hours.

And Zurita resolved to begin with the *Mafalda*. He ordered the anchor to be cast. Then he went below to his cabin, where he wrote a note and, with it in his hand, went across to the cabin occupied by Ichthyander.

"Can you read, Ichthyander? Here's a note for you from Gutiérrez."

Ichthyander quickly opened the note and read the following:

"Ichthyander, please do what I'm going to ask you. There's a sunken ship near the *Jellyfish*. Go down and bring back everything valuable you can find there. Zurita will let you go without your chain but you must come back to the *Jellyfish*. Do this for me, Ichthyander, and you will soon regain your freedom. Gutiérrez."

Ichthyander had never before received any letters from Gutiérrez, so he did not know her handwriting. For a moment he was happy to have received the note but then it suddenly entered his head that it might be another trick of Zurita's.

"Why doesn't she ask for it in person?" Ichthyander said.

"She's not quite well," Zurita replied, "but you'll see her as soon as you're back."

"What does she want with all those valuable things?" Ichthyander asked, still unconvinced.

"You wouldn't have asked that if you had been a real man. Is there a woman who does not want to wear beautiful clothes and expensive jewellery? But that costs money. And there's plenty of it in the sunken ship. It's nobody's now, why not get it for Gutiérrez? What you must do first is find the gold pieces. Look for leather mail bags. Besides, the passengers might wear articles of gold, rings—"

"Do you imagine I'm going to search corpses?" Ichthyander said indignantly. "And then I don't believe you. Gutiérrez is not greedy, she could not have asked me to do a thing like that."

"*Carramba!*" Zurita exploded. He could see his scheme was about to fall through unless he tried some other tack. So he collected himself.

"You're nobody's fool, I can see," he said with a good-humoured laugh. "Well, I'll be frank with you. Here it is. It isn't Gutiérrez who wants the gold from the *Mafalda* but me. Can you believe that?"

Ichthyander couldn't help smiling.

"Rather."

"Fine. You're beginning to believe me, that means we're coming to an understanding. Yes, *I* need that gold. And if you bring me as much gold from the *Mafalda* as your pearls're worth I'll let you go. The trouble is you don't quite trust me, neither do I trust you. I'm afraid to let you go without your chain, for down you go and—"

"If I give you my word to come back I'll keep it."

"So far I've had no chance to test that. You're not exactly fond of me and I'd not be surprised if you didn't keep your word. But you're fond of Gutiérrez and you'd do anything she asked you. Right? So I spoke to her and she was quick to see the point. Of course she wants me to let you go. That's why she wrote the note and gave it to me, wishing to help you on the road to freedom. Is everything clear to you now?"

What Zurita had told Ichthyander seemed to him not only possible but virtually bearing the stamp of truth. The condition about the gold on the *Mafalda* being worth his pearls had escaped him.

Now to compare their worths, calculated Zurita, he'll have to bring—and I'll insist on it —his pile on board my ship. Then I'll have the *Mafalda* gold, the pile and Ichthyander himself all in my hands.

But Ichthyander had no way of knowing what was passing in Zurita's mind. Zurita's seeming frankness had won him over and Ichthyander, after a minute's thought, agreed.

Zurita heaved a sigh of relief.

He won't cheat me, he thought.

"Let's go, quick!"

They both hurried up on deck and Ichthyander jumped straight overboard.

The crew, seeing Ichthyander jump overboard unchained, immediately realized he had gone for the *Mafalda* riches. The idea that Zurita was going to grab it all for himself goaded them into action.

Just as the sailors attacked Zurita, Ichthyander reached the upper deck of the wrecked ship.

Through a huge hatch and down a companion ladder that looked like the staircase of a big building, Ichthyander glided into a spacious alleyway. There it was dark. The only spots of faint light were some open doors along it.

Ichthyander swam through one of these doors and found himself in a lounge. The big port-holes illumined dimly the huge hall, which could accommodate a few hundred people at a time. Ichthyander perched on the sumptuous centre chandelier and had a good look round. It was an eerie sight. All round him against the ceiling swayed chairs and small tables. A grand piano, its lid raised, stood on the small stage, cut into the expanse of soft-carpeted floor. Along one of the walls wainscotted in mahogany that was already warped in places, tubbed palms stretched in a row.

Ichthyander pushed off the chandelier and swam towards the palms. Suddenly he stopped dead: a man was swimming towards him, stopping short as Ichthyander did. A mirror, guessed the amphibian. The huge wall-to-wall mirror duplicated the hall in its dim reflection.

There were no treasures to be found here. Ichthyander swam out into the alleyway, went a deck lower and found himself in a hall, as well-appointed and big as the one above, apparently the restaurant. Scattered on the bar counters and near them were wine bottles, tins, cartons. Most bottles had the corks pushed in by the pressure of the water while some of the tins were almost flattened. Places were laid on the tables but most of the cutlery lay pell-mell on the floor.

Ichthyander headed for the cabins.

Swimming in and out he visited cabins that looked the last word in American comfort. They were all empty. Only in one cabin on the third deck he saw a swollen body, gently rocking near the ceiling.

The passengers must have had time to cast off in boats, he thought.

But down in Third Class, a terrible sight awaited him. The place was cluttered up with bodies of children and adults, men and women, white, Chinese, Negroes, Indians.

Obviously the ship's crew had rushed to the rescue of the First-Class passengers, leaving the rest to fend for themselves. In the resulting stampede, people had pressed round the few exits, crushing each other to death, blocking the way up and to life for others. The doors of some of the cabins were blocked by corpses so that Ichthyander could not manage a look inside.

The water, coming through the open portholes into the long alleyway, gently rocked the bloated corpses. Ichthyander felt frightened and hurried out away from this underwater graveyard.

Surely Gutiérrez didn't know where she was sending me, thought Ichthyander. Surely she couldn't possibly want me to pick the dead men's pockets and rifle their trunks. Of course not. That meant he had again fallen into a trap of Zurita's. So he resolved to come up and demand that Gutiérrez come on deck and confirm her request.

Quick as a fish the young man went up through deck after deck until he was clear of the ship's hull.

He surfaced and swam towards the *Jellyfish.*

"Ahoy, Zurita," he called. "Gutiérrez!"

There was no reply. The silent *Jellyfish* rocked on the waves.

Where have they all gone to? thought the amphibian. What's Zurita up to now? Cautiously, Ichthyander swam towards the schooner and scrambled aboard.

"Hey, Gutiérrez!" he called again.

"Here we are," he heard Zurita's voice that barely reached him from offshore. Ichthyander looked round and saw Zurita, peeping from behind some bushes on the shore.

"Gutiérrez's taken ill. Swim over here, Ichthyander!" he shouted.

She was ill and he would see her. Ichthyander jumped overboard and swam quickly shorewards.

Ichthyander was already clear of the water when he heard Gutiérrez's muffled cry:

"He's lying! Run, Ichthyander!"

The amphibian turned, dived and swam away underwater. When he had put quite a distance between himself and the shore he broke water and looked back. He could just make out something white fluttering on the shore.

Perhaps it was Gutiérrez bidding him farewell. Would he ever see her again?

Quickly Ichthyander swam for the open sea, deserted but for a small vessel, low on the water, heading due south. She churned water open with her sharp bows, leaving behind a foamy wake.

Humans are best left to themselves, thought Ichthyander, and diving steeply, was lost in the sea.

PART III

THE LONG-LOST FATHER

Ever since that unsuccessful trip on. the submarine Baltasar had been in the blackest of moods.

"Damn the whites!" he was saying grumpily one afternoon, sitting all by himself in the shop. "They took our lands from us and made us their slaves. They maim our children and steal our daughters. They want to kill us off, down to the last babe-in-arms."

"Hullo, brother," he heard Cristo's voice. "I've brought news. Big news. Ichthyander's found."

"What?!" Baltasar sprang up from his seat. "Well, go on, for heaven's sake."

"I'll go on if you don't chip in—if you do I'll forget something. He's come back. I was right that time: he was on that wreck."

"Where's he now? At Salvator's?"

"Yes."

"I'll go to Salvator and demand my son back."

"He won't agree," Cristo said. "And he forbids Ichthyander to swim out into the ocean. Sometimes I let him go though—"

"He will! I'll kill him if he won't! Let's go, straightway."

Cristo waved his hands in alarm.

"Wait till tomorrow at least. I'd a hell of a job, I can tell you, getting permission to look up my granddaughter. He's turned so suspicious. He sure sees right into your heart with them eyes of his. Put it off till tomorrow, I say."

"All right. Let it be tomorrow. Today I'll go to the gulf. Perhaps I'll be able to see my son, even if only from afar."

All that afternoon and night Baltasar spent on a cliff over the gulf, peering into the waves. The sea was rough. The cold southerner blew in fierce gusts, carrying foam off wavetops and spraying the cliff with it. Surf pounded the shore. In and out of the racing clouds, the moon threw a fitful light on the waves. Try as he would Baltasar could spot nothing in the seething ocean. Dawn came and found him squatting stock-still on the cliff-top. The ocean was less sombre now but as empty as before.

Then Baltasar stirred. His keen eyes had espied a dark object, bobbing up and down on the waves. A man. Perhaps, a drowned man? No, the man was floating stretched out on his back, his hands behind his head. Could that be *him*?

Baltasar was not mistaken. It was Ichthyander.

The old man rose and, pressing his hands to his chest, shouted, "Ichthyander, my son!" and lifting his arms above his head took a dive.

It was a deep dive and when he broke water the man was gone. Baltasar dived again but then a mammoth roller caught up with him, turned him, tossed him ashore and rolled back with a deep growl.

Baltasar rose, dripping, looked at the waves and sighed.

"Could I have imagined it?"

When the sun and wind had dried his clothes he went off to the great wall of Salvator's estate and knocked on the steel gates.

"Who's there?" a Negro asked peeping at Baltasar through a half-open spy-hole.

"I want to see the doctor on urgent business."

"Doctor's not receiving," the Negro said and slid the spy-hole shut.

Shouting, Baltasar started pounding the gates but they remained closed. The only sound coming from beyond the wall was a fierce barking of dogs.

"Just you wait, you Spanish gallows-bird!" Baltasar threatened and set off for Buenos Aires.

Not far from the Law Courts there was a *pulqueria*, called *La Palmera*, a squat old building with thick white walls. A narrow verandah ran along its front, complete with striped awning, rows of tables and cacti in blue enamelled vases. It was quite a busy place in the evenings; in the daytime the customers preferred the cool low-ceilinged rooms. During court sessions the *pulqueria* was a sort of law court lobby where plaintiffs and defendants, witnesses for the defence and witnesses for the prosecution whiled away hour after tedious hour over a glass of wine or *pulque*. A few bright youngsters shuttle-cocking between the Law Courts and *La Palmera* kept them abreast of the latest developments. This arrangement suited everybody. Shyster attorneys and false witnesses frequented the place in search of customers.

Baltasar's curio trade had brought him more than once to *La Palmera*. He knew he could obtain advice there or get somebody to write a petition for him. So this was where Baltasar bent his steps.

He passed quickly through the verandah into the cool hall where he first drew in a deep breath of cool air and wiped beads of sweat off his brow.

"Larra here?" he asked a boy hovering nearby.

"Don Flores de Larra's here, sitting in his usual place," the boy replied promptly.

The man who went by the pompous name of don Flores de Larra had once been a court clerk, but was dismissed for accepting bribes. Now he had a big clientèle of all those whose cases stood in bad need of expert advice. Baltasar had had dealings with the man before.

Larra was sitting at his table near a broad-silled Gothic window. On the table within easy reach were a wine glass and a bulky brownish attaché case. Always at the ready his fountain-pen peeped from the breast-pocket of his worn olive-coloured suit. Larra was fat, bald, red of cheek and nose, clean-shaven and proud. The light breeze that found its way into the room raised the remnants of his silver hair in a crown. The *Señor* Chief Justice himself could not have been a grander sight.

Seeing Baltasar approach Larra threw him a casual nod and motioned him to a wicker chair opposite his own.

"Pray be seated," he said. "What business brings you here? Would you like some wine? *Pulque*?"

As a rule Larra did the ordering and his client the paying.

Baltasar seemed not to hear him.

"Important business, very important, Larra."

"Don Flores de Larra," the learned in the law corrected him and sipped a little wine.

But Baltasar let that go.

"And what this important business of yours might be?"

"You know, Larra—"

"Don Flores de—"

"Oh, leave your tricks for those who don't know you," Baltasar said with feeling. "This is important business, I tell you."

"Well then, out with it," Larra said in quite a different tone.

"D'you know the 'sea-devil'?"

"Have not had the honour of meeting personally so far but heard a lot about," Larra said, relapsing into his fustian.

"Well, the one that everybody calls the 'sea-devil' is my son Ichthyander."

"But that's impossible!" exclaimed Larra. "You must have been drinking, Baltasar."

The Indian banged his fist on the table.

"I haven't had anything to drink or eat since yesterday—unless you call a few mouthfuls of sea-water a drink."

"Then it's even worse."

"You think I'm loony? No, I'm as clear-minded as can be. Now, shut up and listen to me."

And Baltasar told Larra the whole story. Larra listened to the Indian, deeply engrossed, his grey eyebrows invading his forehead. When the Indian stopped, forgetting all about his grand airs, he slapped the table-top with a fat hand and shouted, *"Mil diablos!"*

A boy in a white apron, a dirty napkin in his hand, ran to the table.

"What can I do for you?"

"Two bottles of iced Sauterne," and turning to Baltasar, Larra said:

"Splendid! That's a peach of a case. Thought

all that up by yourself, have you? To tell you the truth, though, your fatherhood's the weakest point in it."

"You don't believe me?" said Baltasar, flushing with anger.

"There, there, no offence meant, old boy. I'm only speaking as a lawyer, looking at your case with the eye of the law, if you know what I mean, and it's not got very strong legs to stand on, you know—I mean that last point. But we can stand it on stouter legs, I'm sure. Yes. And land a bit of money, too."

"It's not money I need, it's my son," Baltasar retorted.

"Everybody needs money and particularly those who expect an addition to their family, as you do," Larra said sententiously, and screwing up a shrewd eye, continued, "You see, what makes the whole thing almost as safe as houses is that little point about the kind of surgery Salvator's been engaged in. It can be given such a turn that *pesos* will rain out of that money-bag like overripe oranges dropping from a tree in an autumn gale."

Baltasar took a little sip of the wine Larra had poured him out to wet his lips and said:

"I want my son. You must write a summons against Salvator for me."

"Not on your life!" Larra exclaimed, almost

frightened. "Not at this stage anyway, unless you want to botch up the whole thing. The summons can wait."

"Well, what do you advise?" Baltasar asked.

"First," and Larra bent a fat finger, "we'll send Salvator a letter couched in terms of the utmost politeness. We'll tell him we know all about his illegal experiments and operations and would he please pay us a tidy sum of money to avoid it being revealed. One hundred thousand *pesos.* Yes, one hundred thousand and not a *centavo* less."

Larra looked enquiringly at Baltasar. The Indian frowned but didn't say a word.

"Secondly," went on Larra. "When we get the afore-mentioned sum, as I'm sure we will, we'll send Salvator a second letter, more polite, if anything. In it we'll tell him that Ichthyander's real father's been found and that we have irrefutable proofs of the fact. Then we'll tell him that the father is determined to have his son back even if he has to sue Salvator to get him, and that court proceedings may open the public's eye to the way Salvator has muti·lated Ichthyander. However, if Salvator wishes to avoid court proceedings and retain the boy, would he please pay to the persons and at the place and time specified by us the sum of one million *pesos.*"

But Baltasar was not listening. He grabbed a bottle and swung it over the lawyer's head. Larra had never seen him in such a rage.

"Come, come, don't get your monkey up. I was only joking. Come on, put that bottle down," Larra was saying, covering with one hand his shining pate.

"You, you," Baltasar raged, "you suggest that I sell my own son, my Ichthyander! Have you got no heart? Or you're not a human being but a scorpion, a tarantula, and know nothing about a father's feelings!"

"Don't I! Don't I indeed!" Larra shouted back, also roused. "I've got the feelings of five fathers. I've five sons. Five little imps of all sizes. Five mouths to feed. I know, understand and feel everything. You'll get your son. But first have patience and let me finish."

Baltasar calmed down a little. He put the bottle on the table and looked at Larra.

"Well then, go on."

"That's better. So Salvator pays us the sum of one million *pesos*. That'll buy all your Ichthyander needs—and leave a little over for me, for my pains and authorship, a mere hundred thousand *pesos* or so. No need to haggle over it. Salvator'll cough up. I'll lay my head on it, he will. As soon as we have the money—"

"We bring him to court."

"A little more patience. We'll offer the story of a sensational crime to the biggest newspaper concern there is for say twenty or thirty thousand *pesos*—just pocket-money, you know. Perhaps we'll get a slice of the secret police funds as well. Some of them may make their careers on a case like ours, you know. And when we have squeezed Salvator dry, then go to court, yes, by all means, go and speak about your paternal feelings and may Themis herself help you to prove your claim and to receive in your affectionate embraces your long-lost son."

Larra drained his glass at one gulp, banged it on the table and looked triumphantly at Baltasar.

"What do you say to that?"

"I can neither eat nor sleep and here you are advising me to drag out the case to the end of time," Baltasar began.

"But look what you'll get out of it!" Larra cut in hotly. "Millions! Mil-li-ons. Has your brain suddenly stopped working? After all you've lived without Ichthyander these twenty years."

"Yes, I have. But now— Well, write that paper for me."

"Yes, you've really stopped using your brain!" exclaimed Larra. "Come to your senses,

Baltasar! Try to understand! Why, man, it's millions! Money! Gold! You'll have everything money can buy. The best tobacco, cars, schooners, this very *pulqueria*—"

"Write that paper or I go to somebody else," Baltasar said in a final tone of voice.

Larra knew when he was licked. He shook his head sadly, heaved a sigh, took a sheet of paper out of his attaché case and jerked his pen free.

In a few minutes a summons was drawn up in proper form against Salvator for unlawfully seizing and mutilating Baltasar's son.

"I'm telling you for the last time, come to your senses," said Larra.

"Give it here," the Indian said, stretching his hand for the sheet of paper.

"Hand it in to the chief prosecutor. You know where?" Larra instructed his client and muttered under his breath, "May you trip on the steps and break your neck."

Leaving the prosecutor's office Baltasar ran into Zurita on the great white staircase.

"What business brings you here?" asked Zurita, throwing a suspicious glance at Baltasar. "You haven't gone and lodged a complaint against me, have you?"

"Complaints ought to be lodged against the whole lot of you," Baltasar said, meaning the

Spanish, "but there's nobody to lodge 'em with. Where have you hidden my daughter?"

"I'll teach you to keep a civil tongue in your head," flared up Zurita. "Had you not been my wife's father I'd have given you a taste of my stick."

And pushing Baltasar roughly out of his way Zurita went up the steps and disappeared behind the monumental door of stout oak.

A CASE WITHOUT PRECEDENT

The chief prosecutor of Buenos Aires had a rare visitor—His Grace the Bishop Juan de Garcilaso, Dean of the Cathedral.

The prosecutor, fat and dapper, with small bleary eyes, short-cut hair and dyed moustache, came out from behind his desk to meet the bishop. With great care the host seated his dear guest in the heavy leather armchair at his desk.

The unlikeness between host and guest was striking. The prosecutor's red face was fleshy, with thick lips and a big pear-like nose. His stumpy fingers looked not unlike thick sausages, while the buttons on his stomach threatened to be wrenched off any moment by the sheer rise and fall of the imprisoned fat.

Now thinness and paleness were the two

characteristic features of the bishop's face. A thin aquiline nose, a sharp chin and a pair of thin bloodless lips lent him the air of a typical Jesuit. The bishop never looked straight into his interlocutor's eyes, all the same he kept him under sharp observation. The bishop's influence was immense and he willingly took time off from his church affairs for the game of politics.

The greetings over, the bishop came straight to the object of his visit.

"I should like to know," he said softly, "in what stage Professor Salvator's case is?"

"Ah, your Grace," the prosecutor exclaimed amiably, "you are also interested in this case. It's indeed extraordinary, this case," and picking up a fat file and leafing through it he went on, "On Pedro Zurita's denunciation a search was instituted at Professor Salvator's. Zurita's allegation to the effect that Salvator was engaged on unusual operations on animals was fully corroborated. In fact Salvator's gardens have been a real factory of monster animals. It's something fantastic! Salvator, for instance—"

"I know all about the search from the newspapers," the bishop put in softly. "What measures have you taken against Salvator? Is he in custody?"

"Yes, he is. Besides we have seized and taken to town—as Exhibit A and witness for the prosecution—a young man called Ichthyander, known also as the 'sea-devil.' That the notorious 'sea-devil,' the cause of so much trouble to us, should be an inmate of Salvator's zoo! It's amazing! At present a panel of experts, mostly university professors, are conducting an on-the-spot investigation as the zoo proved too big for transportation. But Ichthyander has been brought to town, as I said, and housed in the cellar under the Law Courts. And he's a source of worry, I can tell you. Just imagine, we had to order a big tank for him, for it appears he can't live without water. And, as a matter of fact, he really was in poor condition. Apparently Salvator had brought about some extraordinary changes in his organism, making him into a kind of amphibian. Our experts are now tackling this question."

"I'm more interested in Salvator himself," the bishop said as softly as before. "Under what article of the law is he punishable? And what is your opinion on whether he will be really sentenced?"

"The case of Salvator is extraordinary in that it has no precedent," said the prosecutor. "Frankly speaking I have not yet decided under which article of the law his crime comes. The easiest thing, of course, would be to charge him with carrying out illegal vivisections and disfiguring this young man...."

There was a suggestion of a frown on the bishop's brow.

"So you consider that there is no *corpus delicti* in Salvator's doings?"

"There must be, but what exactly?" the prosecutor said. "Another statement bearing on the subject was handed to me from an Indian called Baltasar. He claims that Ichthyander's his son. His proofs are rather weak but still we could perhaps call him as a witness for the prosecution provided the experts find that Ichthyander is really his son."

"Do you mean to say that at the most Salvator will be charged with violating professional ethics and tried only for operating on a child without obtaining his parents' consent?"

"Yes and, perhaps, for mutilation inflicted. And that's far worse. But there's another angle to this matter from which it might appear in an altogether different aspect. The experts are inclined to believe—very tentatively so far—that a normal mind could never have conceived the mere idea of such monstrous operations on animals, and still less on a human being. They might declare Salvator mentally deranged."

His thin lips compressed in a line and his eyes fixed on a corner of the table, the bishop sat in silence.

"I did not expect this from you," he finally broke silence in a low voice.

"I beg your pardon, your Grace?" the prosecutor said, taken aback.

"Even you, limb of the law, seem to be condoning Salvator's doings, trying to find some justification for his operations."

"But are they really so bad?"

"And hesitating to define the *corpus delicti*. The court of our Holy Catholic Church—the court of Heaven—takes a different view of Salvator's doings. Allow me to come to your aid and offer you advice."

"I'm listening," said the abashed official.

The bishop began in a low voice, gradually working it up to a higher pitch, as if pontifying from the pulpit against atheistic science.

"You seem to think that Salvator's doings are not without some justification. You seem to imply that the human being and the animals he has disfigured now have some advantages they didn't enjoy before. What does this mean? Does this mean that the Creator did not make man the perfect creature he is? Does this mean that a Professor Salvator is free to meddle with His divine will and introduce adjustments into man?"

The host sat listening to the dignitary of the Church, subdued and surprised: he had not expected to be turned from prosecutor to defendant.

"Have you forgotten what the Holy Bible says in the Book of Genesis, Chapter 1, verse 26, 'And God said, Let us make man in our image, after our likeness' and later, verse 27, 'So God created man in his *own* image'? Salvator dares to disfigure this image and likeness and you—even you—find this justifiable!"

"Forgive me, *Padre*," was all the prosecutor could utter.

"Didn't the Lord find His creation perfect," the bishop went on, warming to his subject, "wanting in nothing? You remember well the articles of the laws of man but you forget the articles of the laws of God. Recall to your mind verse 31 of the same chapter of the Book of Genesis, 'And God saw every thing that he had made, and, behold, *it was* very good.' And your Salvator, in his godless vanity, considers that there is room for improvement, that man should be made an amphibian, and you just marvel at it and find justification for it. Isn't that blasphemy? Isn't that a sacrilege? Or do our civic laws no longer punish crimes against God? Have you stopped to think what would happen if everybody said after you that man was miscreated by God and should be turned over to Salvator for remaking? What outrageous aberration this would lead to? God found everything that he had made—all his creatures—very good. And Salvator sets to and transplants animals' heads and skins and creates ungodly monsters, as if mocking the Creator. And you find it difficult to detect a *corpus delicti* in his doings?"

The bishop stopped. Pleased with the effect his speech was having on the prosecutor, he kept silent for a moment and started off again, first in a low voice, then gradually raising the pitch:

"I've said that I am more interested in what will happen to Salvator. But can I be indifferent to what will happen to Ichthyander? Why, this creature hasn't even a Christian name, for after all Ichthyander is only a combination of the Greek words for man and fish. But even granted that Ichthyander is not to blame, being only a victim, he's still a creature begotten of a sacrilege. The mere fact of his existence may lead humble ones into temptation, induce them to entertain blasphemous doubts and even cause to waver those not strong in their faith. Ichthyander must go! The best thing for that unfortunate youth would be to be summoned to Heaven as unfit to live,"—here the bishop threw a meaningful glance at his host. "In any case he should be condemned and shut off from all contact. After all he did commit punishable offences. He stole fish from the fishermen, damaged their nets until, you will remember, he had them so scared that they stopped fishing and the town was left without its supplies. The impious Salvator and his wicked handiwork are a challenge to God and our Holy Church! And the Church will not rest until they are destroyed!"

The bishop went on with his peroration. The prosecutor sat crestfallen, his gaze fixed on the ground, not daring to stem the torrent of wrathful words.

When finally the bishop stopped the prosecutor rose and approached the dignitary of the Church.

"As a Christian," he said in a hollow tone of voice, "I'll bring my sin to my Father confessor for penance. As a law officer I tender you my gratitude for the help you have rendered me. My eyes have been opened to Salvator's crime. He will be tried and convicted. And neither will the sword of Nemesis miss Ichthyander."

Though in custody Dr. Salvator had not knuckled under. He was as calm and dominating as ever, speaking to the investigator and experts in the condescending accents of an adult addressing a bunch of children. His active nature could not stand idleness. He did a great deal of writing and performed a few brilliant operations in the prison hospital. Among others he operated on the prison governor's wife for a malignant tumour and saved her life when she had been given up by all other doctors.

The day of the trial came.

The huge Court was packed, those who had not been able to get inside overflowing the corridors, the square in front of the Law Courts, looking in at the open windows or climbing up the trees for a better view.

Salvator sat in the prisoner's dock with the calm and dignified demeanour of a judge. Everybody's eyes were glued on him. The fact that he was going to conduct his own defence only whipped up the audience's interest.

Ichthyander would, of course, have come in for his share of popular interest but he was not in Court. With the approach of the trial he had been spending more and more time in his water tank, owing to his poor health and everybody's morbid staring. Besides, in the Salvator case Ichthyander was only a witness for the prosecution, rather in the nature of material evidence, as the chief prosecutor had put it, and his own case was to come up for trial later and separately. It had been arranged that way to meet the bishop's wish for a speedy conviction for Salvator. Meanwhile evidence against Ichthyander could be prepared. The prosecutor's agents were paying visits to the *pulqueria La Palmera*, cautiously but busily recruiting witnesses for the future trial. However, the bishop kept hinting broadly to the prosecutor that by far the best for the unfortunate youth would be to depart this life–and furnish ample proof that a man's hand could only spoil what God had made.

Speaking on behalf of the experts' panel Arturo Stein, Professor of Anatomy at the University and an eminent scientist, gave evidence that was listened to with unabated attention.

"On instruction of the Court," he began, "we examined the animals and the young man called Ichthyander that had all been operated upon by Professor Salvator. We also examined his small but well-appointed surgery and laboratories. In his work Professor Salvator made extensive use not only of the latest techniques, such as electric dissection and ultraviolet disinfection, but also of a number of instruments unknown to modern plastic surgery. These apparently were made for him according to his own designs. I do not intend to dwell at any length on Professor Salvator's experiments on animals. In a nutshell, they consisted of a series of operations as daring in conception as they were brilliant in execution. He transplanted tissues, whole organs and limbs, sewed two animals together, changed monorespiratory animals into duorespiratory and vice versa, transformed females into males and experimented in rejuvenation. In Salvator's orchards we also found children of different Indian tribes ranging in age from a few months to fourteen years."

"What was the state you found them in?" asked the prosecutor.

"All the children were in excellent condition. Indeed they looked quite happy. Many of them owed Salvator their very lives. The Indians believed in him and brought him their children from far afield."

A sigh was heard in the hushed hall.

The prosecutor began to fidget. Now that he had got his cue from the bishop the expert's warm words jarred upon his ears.

"Are you going to suggest that the operations the accused carried out served any justifiable purpose?" he asked the expert.

But the presiding judge, a stern-faced silver-haired man, fearing lest the expert answer in the affirmative, hastened to interpose.

"The Court is not interested in the expert's personal opinions on scientific matters. Please proceed, Professor. What were your findings as to the young man Ichthyander of the Araucanian tribe?"

"We found that this body was covered with man-made scales," Professor Stein continued, "of some unknown material, easy to bend but hard to pierce. We are still awaiting the results of its analysis. When swimming Ichthyander used a pair of goggles fitted with special flint glass with an index of refraction near two which enabled him to see better underwater. When we removed the scales we detected a round hole about four inches in diameter under each shoulder-blade covered with five thin strips, the whole looking similar to a shark's gills."

A muffled exclamation of surprise was heard in the hall.

"Yes," the expert continued, "surprising as it must seem, Ichthyander possesses both human lungs and a shark's gills. That is why he can live both on land and in water."

"An amphibian?" the prosecutor said ironically.

"Yes, in fact a human amphibian."

"But how could Ichthyander come to have a shark's gills?" asked the presiding judge.

The expert spread his arms abroad.

"That is a puzzle to which only Professor Salvator holds the answer," he said. "I shall try, however, to sum up our opinion for you. According to the biogenetic law of Haeckel the organism in its development is to a great extent an epitome of the form-modifications undergone by the successive ancestors of the species in the course of their historic evolution. So it can be safely said that man's distant forebears once breathed with their gills."

The prosecutor half-rose in his seat to protest but was motioned back by the presiding judge.

"Here's some embryology to support it. By the twentieth day an embryonic skull shows a set of four parallel ridges, the so-called visceral arches. But later the human foetus's would-be gills undergo a transformation: the first visceral arch develops into the acoustic duct with the ossicles and the Eustachian tube, its lower part turning into the lower jaw; the second arch develops into the hyoid bone; the third into the body and two processes of the thyroid cartilage. This is the normal development and we do not consider that Professor Salvator could have arrested it in the case of Ichthyander. There are on record cases of even adults having an unclosed gill-cleft on the throat directly under the lower jaw, the so-called branchial fistula, but there can be no question of their breathing through them. Had there been, however, any interference with the normal development, the gills would have developed at the expense of the organ of hearing and other functions, making Ichthyander into a monster half-fish. But Ichthyander is a normally developed young man with good hearing, a well-pronounced lower jaw and sound lungs, and besides he has full-grown gills. How Ichthyander's gills and lungs function, what their interaction is, if any, whether his gills get their water via the mouth and lungs or through the two small orifices we discovered on his body directly above each gill-opening—we do not know. Nor could we answer these questions without an autopsy. This is, I repeat again, a puzzle for the solution of which we have to refer to Professor Salvator. Only Professor Salvator can explain to us the origin of the dog-like jaguars and other such animals as well as of the amphibious monkeys, Ichthyander's doubles."

"What is you general conclusion?" asked the presiding judge.

The expert, himself a well-known surgeon, said simply:

"Frankly speaking I can't make head or tail of it. I can only say that what Professor Salvator did, nobody but a man of genius could do. But it does look as if Professor Salvator, on reaching his consummate degree of skill, decided that he could take humans or animals to pieces and put them together in any manner or arrangement he thought best. And though he has been doing this, and with brilliance, nonetheless his daring and scope border on what I'm forced to say looks like insanity."

At this Salvator gave a little contemptuous smile. He had no idea that the experts had resolved to alleviate his lot by pleading his insanity.

"I do not want to produce the impression that such is our considered opinion," the speaker said, catching sight of Salvator's smile, "but we do suggest the accused be submitted to expert medical examination."

"The Court will consider your insanity plea in due time," said the presiding judge. "Professor Salvator, do you intend to give the

Court any explanations of the questions raised by the experts and the prosecutor?"

"Yes," Salvator said. "I do, and I also intend to make it my last word."

SALVATOR'S EXPLANATION

Salvator had risen in his seat and was now running his eye over the hall as if trying to locate somebody. In the front row he saw the bishop and let his sweeping eye stop for a moment, while a faint smile skimmed his lips, before running it farther back, picking out, as he did so, Baltasar, Cristo and Zurita. Then he started to scan the audience again, more careful this time.

"I can't see my victim in Court," he said finally.

"I'm your victim!" Baltasar shouted all of a sudden, jerking up from his seat and resuming it only after a sharp tug administered by Cristo.

"What victim do you mean?" said the presiding judge. "If you mean the animals you have maimed the Court has decided against exhibiting them here. As far as the human amphibian is concerned, he's in the Court building."

"I mean God," Salvator said in an earnest, quiet voice.

On hearing that the presiding judge fell back in his chair in consternation. Has Salvator suddenly gone mad, he thought, or is he perhaps feigning insanity to escape prison?

"Whatever do you mean?" he asked.

"I expect that should be clear to the Court," said Salvator. "Who's the principal and only victim in the present case? Obviously God. According to the prosecution my work has undermined His authority by making what are alleged to be inroads on His domain. He likes what He created, then up comes a doctor and says, 'This is bad; that ought to be altered,' and starts altering what God did according to his own lights."

"This is blasphemy! I want the exact words of the accused put on record," the prosecutor interposed with the air of a man whose sacred feelings have been violated.

Salvator shrugged his shoulders.

"I'm only summing up what it says in the indictment. Isn't that just what it boils down to? At first I was only charged with carrying out vivisections and causing disfigurement. Now another charge is being lined up against me, that of sacrilege. What wind has blown that in? Not from the direction of the Cathedral, by any chance?" and Salvator looked straight at the bishop.

"You have only yourselves to blame for having built up a case where prosecution relies on God as a plaintiff while Charles Darwin shares the prisoner's dock with me. Perhaps I'm wounding the feelings of some people present here, but I will say once again that the organisms of animals and even of man are not perfect and can, indeed, do with improvement. I expect the bishop Juan de Garcilaso here in Court will bear me out on this."

This caused quite a rustle in the hall.

"In 1915, in fact very shortly before I left for the front," Salvator went on, "I happened to effect a slight improvement in the worthy bishop's organism by cutting out his appendix, that useless and risk-ridden appendage of the caecum or, in popular parlance, blind gut. On my surgeon's table my priestly patient did not raise any objections to the sacrilege I was about to commit by cutting out part of his body made after God's image. Can you deny that?" Salvator asked the bishop looking straight at him.

Juan de Garcilaso, a faint flush mounting to his pallid features, sat stock-still, his thin fingers, clenched in his lap, trembling slightly.

"And wasn't there another case at the time

I still had my practice? Hadn't I a visit, and a request to be rejuvenated, from our respected prosecutor, Sr. Augusto de–"

The prosecutor leapt up in protest but his words were drowned in loud laughter.

"I would ask you to keep to the subject, please," the presiding judge said with asperity.

"That would be best asked of the indictment's authors," said Salvator. "It was they who gave this turn to the case in the first place. Apparently certain people here cannot reconcile themselves to the idea that they, like everybody else, are monkeys or even fishes able to speak and hear only because their gill arches have developed into organs of hearing and speaking. Well, not exactly monkeys or fishes, to be sure, but their close descendants," and turning to the prosecutor, who was showing all signs of impatience, Salvator said, "Calm yourself; I do not propose to give a talk here on the theory of evolution." Then, after a pause, he went on, "The trouble with man is not that he has descended from the animal, but that he has not ceased to be an animal, vicious, rude, unintelligent. My learned colleague could have spared you his frightening discourse on embryonic development. For I have never had recourse to influencing embryos or

251

crossing animals, for that matter. I'm a surgeon and a surgeon's knife has always been my only instrument. Surgery often involves transplantation. So, to try and improve on the methods used, I started experimenting on animals. My ultimate aim was the replacement of man's diseased organs and limbs.

"The operated animals I kept in my laboratory, studying the behaviour of organs and limbs often transplanted into environments entirely new for them. When my observations were over, the animals were transferred to the garden. This is the way my zoological gardens came to be built up. I was especially keen on transplanting tissues and organs between far-removed species, those of fishes and mammals, for instance. And in this particular field I've achieved what contemporary scientists still think impossible. But is it, really? I hold that what I alone can do today the run of surgeons will be doing tomorrow. Professor Stein perhaps knows of the latest operations performed by the German surgeon Sauerbruch, who succeeded in substituting a sound shin-bone for a diseased thigh-bone."

"Yes, but what about Ichthyander?" asked the expert.

"Ah Ichthyander, now Ichthyander's my special pride. In his case the difficulty lay not so much in the technique as in the need to change the major functions of a human organism. Half a dozen monkeys were sacrificed in preliminary work before I became quite satisfied in my own mind that I could safely operate on a child."

"What was the nature of the operation?" asked the presiding judge.

"I transplanted a young shark's gills onto a child which enabled him to live both on land and in water."

There were exclamations of surprise among the audience. The reporters present rushed outside to phone the news to their editors.

"Later on I was even able to improve on my original success. The amphibious monkey—my latest result—can live indefinitely long in either element at no risk to health. Now Ichthyander cannot stay outside water for more than three, or, at the most, four days in succession. Long stays on land tend to overtax his lungs and dry up his gills, the first sign of this being shooting pains in his sides. Unfortunately in my absence Ichthyander went off his regimen. He used his lungs a great deal too often with grievous results. The balance is upset and the amphibious man is turning into a human fish. In his present condition he has to spend most of his time in the water."

"How did you arrive at the idea of creating an amphibious man and what was your object in doing so?" the prosecutor said, having asked for and received the judge's permission.

"The same idea prompted me: that man is not perfect. Having gained a great deal through evolution as compared to his animal ancestors man has lost much in the process. Living in the water, for instance, would provide an immense advantage for man. And indeed, why shouldn't he enjoy this advantage? We know from the theory of evolution that all the land animals now existing have evolved from water animals. And we also know that some of the land animals went back later. The dolphin was a fish originally, then came on land and became a mammal, only to return to the water later though remaining a mammal, just like the whale. They both breathe with lungs. A dolphin can also be made into an amphibian. In fact that's what Ichthyander was asking of me so that his friend— a dolphin—could stay longer with him underwater. And I was going to perform the necessary operation. Ichthyander—the first fish among men and the first man among fish—

couldn't help feeling lonely. Now it would be quite different if many more people followed his example. That mighty element—water—would then lie conquered at man's feet. I'd like to give you a glimpse of its might. As much as three-quarters of the earth is covered by water. But that's only surface. Men could settle the ocean in layers. Thousands of millions of men would have ample accommodation as well as an inexhaustible supply of food and raw materials close to hand.

"And take the ocean's power potential. It is a known fact that the ocean waters take up the equivalent of 79,000 million HP in solar energy. But for air heating and other leakages the ocean would have been boiling long ago. What use does man put this practically unlimited store of energy to? Almost none at all.

"And what about the power of ocean currents? The Gulf Stream and the Florida Current alone carry between them 91,000 million tons of water per hour, about 3,000 times as much as a major river. Add to this the power of the other ocean currents. What use does man put this power to? Again almost none.

"And what about the power of ocean waves

and tides? You should know that a wave can have a striking force of three and a half tons per square foot, can reach as high as 142 feet and lift with it as much as one thousand tons, say, of rocks; that the highest tides touch the fifty-five-foot mark. What use does man put these forces to? Once again almost none.

"On land man cannot go very high above the Earth's surface or very deep below it. In the ocean life goes on everywhere—from North Pole to South, from surface to bottom.

"What use do we put all this unlimited wealth to? We catch fish—and that only goes skin-deep, as it were, leaving the greater depths untapped; we collect sponges, coral, pearls, weeds—and that's about everything.

"We do some submarine work by way of erecting piers for bridges and dams and refloating sunken ships. And even that is done at the expense of hard work and risk, and often loss of life. But then what can you really expect of man if two minutes underwater is enough to kill him?

"Now it would be quite a different proposition if man could live and work underwater. Without diving suits or canned oxygen. The

fabulously rich deposits he would then discover-
er! Ichthyander told me once—no, I don't
want to conjure up the ogre of human avarice.
He used to bring me samples of rare metals
and ores he picked up on the sea-bed. The
samples were small but the deposits might have
been immense.

"And what about sunken treasures? It will
suffice to recall the tragic fate of the *Lusitania*
sunk by a German submarine off the Irish
coast in 1915. Apart from the valuables
the fifteen hundred passengers might have had
on themselves the *Lusitania* carried in her
strongroom gold coin to the tune of 150 million dollars and 50 million dollars' worth of
bullion. *(Exclamations in the Court.)* Besides,
there were two cases of diamonds on board
the ship bound for Amsterdam. The consign-
ment included one of the world's largest bril-
liants, the Caliph, worth many millions of dollars. Of course, even a man like Ichthyander
could not descend to such depths; to do this
a man would have to be created (*this drew
a snort of indignation from the prosecutor*),
capable of withstanding high pressure like
deep-water fish. And this is not impossible.
Just a matter of time."

"You seem to assume the role of an omnipo-
tent god," said the prosecutor.

Paying no attention to his words Salvator went on:

"If man could live underwater the ocean would be his for the asking. It would cease to claim its heavy toll of life and property and we would no longer have to mourn our lost at sea."

Salvator's audience, compelled by his eloquence, seemed to see a vision of an underwater world conquered by man. Even the presiding judge succumbed to the spell.

"Then why didn't you publish the results of your experiments?" he asked.

"I was in no particular hurry to get into the dock," Salvator said with a smile, "and then I was afraid that, our social system being what it is, my discoveries might bring more harm than good. As it was, a tussle started round Ichthyander. Who informed against me after all? Zurita, who wanted to take his revenge on me when Ichthyander had slipped through his hands. And from Zurita Ichthyander would have been taken by their Lordships the Admirals and trained to sink warships. No, I could not make Ichthyander—and other Ichthyanders—public property in a country where greed and struggle for survival turn the greatest discoveries into something evil, only adding to the amount of human suffering. I thought of—"

Salvator stopped short. When he started again it was in quite a different tone of voice. "I'm going to leave that unsaid, I think. Otherwise I might be again styled insane," he said with a smile and looked at the experts. "And that's an honour I'd like to renounce herewith, even were the word genius tagged onto it. I'm not a madman, nor am I a maniac. I've done what I set out to do, haven't I? You've seen it all. If you find my actions criminal it's up to you to try me and convict me. I beg for no leniency."

IN PRISON

Acting on the instruction of the Court the experts examined the state of Ichthyander's mental ability. They found he had great difficulty answering the simplest questions. Even when asked about the year, month or day Ichthyander kept answering, "I don't know." Yet, the experts were hesitant to declare him mentally deficient, for they realized that the state of his mind was due to his exceptional background and that the scope of his knowledge was bound to be limited. "Not responsible for his actions" was what they finally agreed on.

And that made him unamenable to the law. The case against him was dropped and a guardianship suggested. Promptly two persons came forward: Zurita and Baltasar.

Salvator had been right in saying that Zurita had informed against him to get his revenge. But that was only part of the story. Zurita wanted Ichthyander back in his hands and saw the guardianship as an easy shortcut to that end. Zurita had not stopped at the expense of bribing the officials in charge with a dozen of his finest pearls and was now awaiting results in smug confidence.

Baltasar had claimed natural guardianship rights. But that was throwing straws against the wind. In spite of Larra's efforts the experts refused to consider his client's paternity on the strength of one witness, a brother of Baltasar's at that

Larra was not aware of the backstage influences in the case. Baltasar as plaintiff, as father robbed of his son, had been useful at Salvator's trial; Baltasar as Ichthyander's guardian ran counter to the interests of the Law and the Church.

Cristo who was now living at his brother's was greatly worried about Baltasar. The old Indian would sit motionless for hours at a stretch, forgetting about food and sleep, then suddenly start rushing about the shop in a frenzy of excitement, shouting, "My son! My son!" and hurling abuse at everything Spanish.

One day after another of such fits Baltasar said to Cristo:

"I'm going to the prison, brother. I'll give my best pearls to the jailors so they let me see my son. I'll speak to him. He'll know I'm his father. A son *will* know his father. My blood's sure to speak up in him."

Try as he would Cristo could not dissuade his brother. Baltasar was adamant.

In prison he entreated some guards, wept at the feet of others, giving pearls to all till he finally got inside Ichthyander's cell.

The small cell scantily illumined through the slit of a barred window was stuffy and smelly: the jailors didn't bother to change the water in the tank often enough, nor did they carry away the fish offal the strange prisoner left after his meals.

Baltasar approached the tank and looked at the dark mirror of the water's surface.

"Ichthyander!" he called softly, and again, "Ichthyander!" but apart from a slight ripple on the surface nothing happened.

Baltasar waited a little, then stretched out a shaky hand and dipped it into the tepid water. It struck a shoulder. Instantly Ichthyander's head popped out of the tank, followed by his shoulders.

"Who are you? What do you want?"

Baltasar sank onto his knees and stretching out his arms began rapidly:

"Ichthyander, your father's come to you. Your real father. Salvator isn't. Salvator's an evil man. He disfigured you. Ichthyander! Look at me closely. You know I'm your father, don't you?"

Water trickled in slow drops out of Ichthyander's thick hair onto his pale face and down off his chin. His gaze was fixed on the old Indian, wistful and quizzical.

"I don't know you," he said.

"Ichthyander," cried Baltasar, "look again!" and, suddenly, clutching Ichthyander's head, he pressed it to himself and started kissing it frenziedly, sobbing aloud.

Trying to escape the unexpected caresses Ichthyander splashed about in the tank, sending little eddies spilling over the rim onto the floor. All of a sudden a strong hand took Baltasar by the scruff of his neck, lifted him up bodily and threw him aside He struck his head against the wall and slumped down.

When he opened his eyes it was to see Zu-

rita towering over him, his right hand balled
into a fist, his left flourishing a sheet of paper
in triumph.

"See this? It's the guardianship order. You'll
have to hunt elsewhere for a rich son for yourself. As to the young man here I take him
home with me tomorrow. Got that?"

From where he lay huddled up against the
wall Baltasar growled menacingly. The next moment, with a savage yell, he was up and at
his enemy. Snatching the order out of Zurita's
hand and stuffing it into his mouth, he
went on hitting out at the Spaniard. Zurita
hit back.

The jailor, who witnessed the fight from the
doorway, felt that the moment demanded the
strictest neutrality; they both had been liberal
in greasing his palm and he wanted to be
loyal to both. So it wasn't until Zurita started
throttling Baltasar in dead earnest that the
jailor stirred to action.

"There, there, don't strangle him."

However, deaf with rage, Zurita was pressing on his advantage and there's no saying
how it would have ended had a familiar voice
not called out at that point.

"*Señor* guardian priming himself for his
new duties—splendid!"

"Well, what are you standing there for?

Don't you know your duties?" Salvator rapped at the two jailors for all the world as if he were the governor of the place.

Salvator's words had immediate effect: the jailors rushed to drag the men apart. The noise attracted more jailors and soon order was restored.

Even in prison, even in face of a sure conviction, Salvator had retained his strength of spirit and his ability to command.

"Take them away," he ordered. "I want to be left alone with Ichthyander."

And the jailors complied. In spite of their noisy protests Zurita and Baltasar were taken away and the door shut.

When the clatter of boots had died away Salvator went across to the tank.

"Come out of there, Ichthyander," he told the amphibian who had just looked out of the water. "I want to examine you."

Ichthyander did as he was told.

"Nearer to the light," Salvator went on, "that's it. Breathe in and out. Deeper. Once more. Stop breathing. That's it," he said as he tapped Ichthyander's chest and listened to his irregular breathing.

"Short of breath, aren't you?"

"Yes, Father," said Ichthyander.

"You've got only yourself to blame, you know," said Salvator. "You shouldn't have stayed on land for so long at a time."

Ichthyander dropped his head and was lost in thought for a moment. Then he suddenly looked up straight into Salvator's eyes.

"But why, Father?" he asked. "Why does everybody else live on land and I can't?"

Salvator had more difficulty meeting that gaze, full of hidden reproach, than answering questions in Court. But he didn't turn his eyes away.

"Because you possess what nobody else possesses: the ability to live under the water," he said. "Supposing you had the option of becoming like everybody else here on land or living only in the ocean. What would you choose?"

"I don't know," Ichthyander drawled, after a moment's thought. The ocean and the land—meaning Gutiérrez—were equally dear to him, but Gutiérrez was lost for him now.

"The ocean, I should say," he said.

"As a matter of fact you've chosen it already—by your disobedience. Now that the balance in your body's upset it's only the ocean for you, I'm afraid."

"The ocean, yes, but not this horrible tank, Father. I'll die here! Oh, if only I could be back in the ocean!"

"I'll do my best to see you delivered from prison as soon as possible," Salvator said, smothering a sigh. "Keep a stiff upper lip, my boy," and tapping on his shoulder by way of encouragement Salvator went out.

Back in his cell he sat down on the stool at the narrow table and fell into meditation.

Like any other surgeon he knew the bitter taste of failure. Quite a few people had died under his knife before he had attained his present skill. Yet his mind was not burdened by memories. Dozens had died to save thousands. He found the ratio comforting.

Now this was different. Ichthyander was his special pride. In Ichthyander he loved his best achievement. Besides, he had grown fond of the boy over the years and looked on him as his own son. So he sat there, worried, thinking about Ichthyander's present condition and what the future held for him.

Somebody knocked at the door.

"Come in," said Salvator.

"I'm not intruding, Professor?" the governor said in a low voice as he came in.

"Not at all," Salvator said, rising. "How are your wife and child?"

"Very well, thank you. I've sent them to my wife's mother, way in the Andes."

"That's right, mountain air is just the thing for them," said Salvator. Throwing a glance at the door the governor came closer to Salvator.

"I owe you my wife's life, Professor," he began, his voice still lower. "I love her. I can't–"

"No thanks are needed. I only did my duty."

"I'll always feel I'm deeply in your debt," said the governor. "And it's not only that. I've got no education to speak of, but I read my newspaper and I know Professor Salvator's worth. If you ask me, a person like you oughtn't to be in prison, together with thieves and tramps."

"As far as I know," Salvator said with a smile, "my learned colleagues are doing their hardest to get me transferred to a padded cell."

"An asylum is still a prison," the governor retorted, "and even worse. Instead of thieves you'll have lunatics for mates. No, that mustn't happen," and lowering his voice to a whisper, he said, "It's not only for their health I send my family into the mountains. This is what I decided. I'll help you escape and will cut and run myself. Need made me take my job but I hate it. They won't find me; as for you, you'll leave the country. There's something more I wanted to tell you," he added after some hesitation. "I'm giving away an official secret, a state secret—"

"You needn't do that," Salvator interrupted him.

"Yes, but . . . I can't . . . for one thing, I can't carry out the horrid order I've received. My conscience would give me no rest all my life. And it's all right when I think it's you I'm giving it away to. You've done such a lot for me, and the authorities—I owe nothing to them, still less so they're forcing a crime on me."

"Are they?" was all Salvator said.

"Yes; I learned they are not going to give Ichthyander to either Baltasar or Zurita for all him being the guardian and the bribe money it's cost him. They're going—they're going to kill Ichthyander."

Salvator started slightly.

"Is that so? Go on!"

"Yes, kill him. That's what the bishop has been after all the time, though, I suppose, he never said it in so many words. They've given me the poison, potassium cyanide, I think they called it. Tonight I'm to spill it into Ichthyander's tank. The prison doctor's in on it. He'll certify death was caused by the operation you performed when making Ichthyander into an amphibian. If I don't do it it'll go real hard for me. And I've got a family to support. They've got me right where they want me, you see. I slipped up in the past—nothing serious though. Almost accidental. If I do it, they'll shut me up for good later, no doubt. Anyhow my mind's made up; I'm running away. I can't and won't kill Ichthyander. To save both of you—at such short notice—is impossible. But I *can* save you. I've thought of everything. I'm sorry for Ichthyander but your life's more valuable. You'll create another Ichthyander, by your skill, but nobody in the world could create another Salvator."

When he finished, Salvator shook the man's hand and said:

"Thank you, but I can't expose you to all this danger for my own sake—"

"There's no danger. I've thought of everything."

"Wait a minute. I can't accept this for my own sake. But if you agreed to save Ichthyander you'd be doing more for me than saving myself. I'm full of health and sure to find friends to help me out of prison. But Ichthyander must be freed without delay—all the more so because of what you've just told me."

"I'll do as you wish," said the governor.

Left alone, Salvator smiled and said:

"Good. That'll snatch the bone of contention away right under everybody's nose."

For some time Salvator was walking up and down the cell, then he went up to the table, wrote something on a sheet of paper, got up and knocked several times on the door.

"Please ask the governor to come to me."

When the governor came Salvator said to him:

"There's another thing I wanted to ask of you. Could you possibly arrange for me to visit Ichthyander today, for the last time?"

"Why, nothing could be easier. No authorities around, the whole prison's at your disposal."

"Splendid. And there's one thing more."

"I'm at your service."

"In freeing Ichthyander you'll be doing me an immense service—"

"But you, Professor, you've done a lot for me, too."

"All right, we'll consider we're quits," Salvator interrupted him. "Now, I want to help your family. Here, take this note. It's just an address, signed with the letter 'S' for Salvator. If you're ever in need of shelter or money remember the address. You can trust the man."

"But—

"No buts, please. Now take me to Ichthyander."

Ichthyander was surprised to see Salvator entering his cell for a second time that day. He was even more surprised when he caught his glance, at once sad and tender as never before.

"Ichthyander, my son, listen to me," said Salvator. "We're going to part soon, sooner than I expected, and perhaps for very long. You'll get your freedom tonight but I'm still worried about you. If you stay here you might become the slave of Zurita or some other brute like him—"

"But what about you, Father?"

"I'll be convicted, of course, and tucked away for a stretch of two or more years. You must tide over it in a place both safe and far away. There is such a place, but very far from here, beyond South America, on one of the Tuamotu or Low Archipelago islands in the Pacific. You'll not find it easy getting there and locating the spot but all the hazards you're likely to encounter will be nothing compared to the risks you'd run dodging your enemies' traps here, in the Rio de la Plata.

"Now about your route. You can get there, travelling round South America, either the southern or the northern way. Both routes have their advantages and disadvantages. The northern route is somewhat longer. Besides, you would have to pass through the Panama Canal, which is dangerous. You may be caught, particularly in the locks, or crushed to death by a ship. The canal is rather narrow and shallow. It is 500 feet at the widest and only 45 feet deep, so that the modern ocean-going vessels all but scrape the bottom with their keels.

"On the other hand, you'd be travelling in warm seas. Besides, three major shipping lines run westwards from the Panama Canal: two of them to New Zealand, the third to the Fiji Islands and farther. Choosing either of the New Zealand lanes and following the ships or even getting a ride on them would bring you almost to your destination. You'd only have to head a little more to the north and you'd be there.

"Now the southern route is shorter but you'd swim in colder waters, near the northernmost ice floes, especially if you went round Cape Horn. And you'd be ill advised to try to negotiate the Strait of Magellan. It's much too stormy. It used to be a veritable graveyard for sailing-ships and is still considered very dangerous, particularly on the western side where it's narrower and reef-ridden. Constant westerners of gale force drive the water before them so you'd have to swim upstream and across whirlpools that even for you might prove fatal.

"And that brings us back to the Cape Horn variant, even if it is longer. There's the cold-water snag, too, but I hope you'll get conditioned as you go and remain in good health. As for food you'll have plenty of that in any part of the ocean.

"And then, of course, it'll be a bit more difficult for you to find your way to the Tuamotu Archipelago from down there than from the Panama Canal. There'll be no busy shipping lines to guide you. But you'll have the place's bearings and will be able to get sun fixes with a set of instruments I made specially for you. I'm afraid they might be quite a burden—"

"I'll take Leading with me. He'll carry anything there is to carry. I don't want to leave him behind, anyway. He must be missing me awfully."

"I wonder who's missing whom worse," Salvator smiled. "Well, that's settled. Splendid. When you get to the Tuamotu Islands, look

18—2785

for a solitary coral-fringed island. You will know it by a long mast with a big fish for a weathercock on its top. You can't miss it. It might take you one, two or even three months to find it but never mind—you'll strike it in the end. The water's warm there and oysters plentiful."

Salvator had taught Ichthyander to listen to what he said patiently, without interrupting, but here Ichthyander could not resist the sudden temptation to ask a question.

"But what shall I find on that island?"

"Friends. Kind and loyal friends," said Salvator. "My old friend, Armand Villebois, the famous French oceanographer, lives there. I got to know and love him many years ago when I was in Europe. He's a most interesting man but there's no time to go into that now. I hope you'll be able to make friends with him yourself and learn the story of what brought him to that lonely atoll in the Pacific. He's far from lonely there though. His wife, a fine woman, and their two children live with him. His daughter was born on the island and should be about seventeen now, his son is older, about 25, I should think.

"They know all about you from my letters and I'm sure will receive you like one of the family—" Salvator stopped short. "You'll have to spend most of your time in the water, of course. But you'll be able to go ashore for a few hours every day. Perhaps, your health permitting, you'll be able in the long run to stay as long on land as in the water.

"Armand Villebois will be like a father to you and you in turn may prove indispensable for him in his scientific work. As it is, you know more about the ocean and its inhabitants than a dozen professors rolled in one." Salvator smiled ironically. "Those cranks of experts questioned you—all according to the usual rigmarole—and you couldn't answer because it didn't happen to concern you. Now had they asked you, say, about the currents, water temperature and salinity in the Rio de la Plata and thereabouts, they would have been able to compile a fat volume of sound science out of your answers. Imagine the amount of facts you could gather—and then pass onto people—were your underwater excursions directed by such a brilliant scientist as Armand Villebois. Between him and you, I'm quite certain of it, you'll produce a work on oceanography that will be a milestone in the development of that science. And your name will stand on the cover side by side with that of Armand Villebois—he'll insist on it, or I don't know him. Here you'd be forced to serve the base interests of igno-rant grabbing people. There you'll be serving science, that means the whole of humanity. And I'm sure that in the clear waters of the lagoon and at the Villebois' you will find a haven and happiness.

"One more piece of advice. As soon as you're in the ocean—and that should be tonight—go home immediately via the tunnel—there's only Jim at home—get the navigation instruments, knife and the rest, find your Leading and start on your way there and then, not even waiting for dawn to break.

"Farewell, Ichthyander, or rather, good-bye."

Salvator embraced and kissed Ichthyander, which he had never done before. Then he smiled, patted Ichthyander on the shoulder, and saying, "You'll make it all right," he left the cell.

THE ESCAPE

Just back from the factory after the day's work Olsen was sitting down to his dinner when there was a knock at the door.

"Who's there?" Olsen shouted resenting the interruption. The door opened to admit Guti-érrez.

"Why, it's Gutiérrez! Well, well!" Olsen

exclaimed, at once surprised and pleased, getting up from his chair.

"Hullo, Olsen," she said. "Go on with your dinner, never mind me," and leaning against the closed door, she said: "I couldn't live any longer with my husband and his mother. Zurita—he dared to strike me. So I left him. I've left him for good, Olsen."

The news made Olsen stop his hand in mid air.

"I must say, this *is* unexpected," he said. "Here, take a seat; you can hardly keep on your feet. But what about that what-God-hath-joined-together-let-no-man-put-asunder thing you told me? So that's over? Good for you. Came back to your father, did you?"

"Father doesn't know about what happened. Zurita's sure to look for me at Father's so I'm staying with a friend of mine."

"Well, what are your plans?"

"I want to get a job. I came to ask you whether you could help me find a job at your factory—any job."

Olsen shook his head worriedly.

"It's not easy at the moment. But, of course, I'll try and do my best for you," he said, and after a pause, added:

"How will your husband take it?"

"I don't care."

"But he will," Olsen said with a smile. "He'll try to run you down. Don't forget you're still in Argentina. When he does he won't let you be, you know. He'll have the law and public opinion on his side, too."

Gutiérrez thought a while and said with de termination:

"Well, what of it? I'll go to Canada, Alaska—"

"Greenland, the North Pole!" Olsen caught her up and, in a serious tone, added, "We'll think about it together. It's not safe for you to stay here, that's for sure. I've been thinking about quitting the place myself. It's a pity we couldn't make it that time. But Zurita kidnapped you and we lost our fares and our money. And I've got a hunch you can't afford your fare to Europe now any more than I can. But then who says we must go straight across the water. If we—I'm stressing 'we,' because I'm not going to leave you before I'm satisfied you're safe—if we get at least across the border into Paraguay, or, still better, into Brazil, Zurita'll find it much more difficult to locate us. And that'll give us enough leeway to prepare for a passage to the States or Europe. Do you know that Dr. Salvator's in prison, and Ichthyander too?"

"Ichthyander? So he's found? Why is he in

prison? Can I see him?" came a salvo of questions.

"Yes, he's in prison and Zurita's been appointed his guardian. You can't imagine what a rotten frame-up the Salvator case was!"

"How terrible! But can't he be saved?"

"I tried my best but it wasn't good enough. Then all of a sudden, I found a powerful ally, the prison governor himself. We're to free Ichthyander tonight. I've just received two notes, one from Salvator, the other from the prison governor."

"I want to see him!" said Gutiérrez. "May I go with you?"

Olsen pondered.

"I don't think you should," he said at last. "Nor should you see him at all, I'm afraid."

"But why?"

"Because he's ill; ill as a man, though all right as a fish if you get me."

"I don't."

"He can't breathe air any longer. Think what will happen if he sees you. He'll want to see a great deal more of you, but life on land can only kill him."

Gutiérrez hung her head.

"Well, you must be right, I suppose—" she said, after a long pause.

"There's a barrier now—the ocean—between him and the rest of people. His fate's sealed. From now on it's only the ocean for him and nothing but the ocean."

"But how is he to live there, I mean, all alone among all those sea-creatures?"

"He *was* quite happy among them until—"

A blush mounted to Gutiérrez's face.

"He won't be as happy as before, of course."

"Oh, stop it, Olsen," Gutiérrez said sadly.

"Time's a good healer, though. Perhaps he'll regain his former peace of mind and live till ripe old age among all those creatures of the sea, unless a shark brings him an untimely end. And as to death—well, it's the same everywhere."

Twilight had set in outside and the room was dark.

"Well, I must be off," Olsen said, rising from his chair. Gutiérrez also rose.

"But may I at least see him from a distance?" said Gutiérrez.

"Of course, provided you keep there."

"It's a promise."

It was already quite dark when, clad as a

water-carrier, Olsen drove into the prison court through the gates that faced Calle de Coronel Diaz.

The guard challenged him.

"Sea-water for the 'devil'," Olsen answered as the prison governor had taught him.

The guards knew about the prison's unusual inmate—the "sea-devil"—who was kept in a tank full of sea-water as he couldn't stand the tap kind, and were accustomed to the sight of the water cart.

Olsen drove up to the prison building and round the corner that housed the kitchen and stopped at the staff entrance. The prison end of the matter had already been seen to by the governor. The sentries at the entrance and in the corridor, having been sent away on various pretexts, he walked Ichthyander out into the court.

"Get into the barrel, quick!"

Ichthyander wasted no time.

"Off you go!"

Olsen jerked at the reins, drove out of the prison court and proceeded unhurriedly on his way along Avenida de Alvear and past Retiro Station.

A woman could be seen following the cart at a distance.

It was dark by the time Olsen had cleared the city and taken the road that skirted the beach. The wind was picking up. Surf pounded the shore, breaking noisily against solitary boulders.

Olsen looked around. There was nobody in sight, except for the distant headlights of a town-bound car. He waited for it to pass.

Hooting, the car shot dazzlingly past and was gone.

Now's the time for it, Olsen thought, and turned round to motion Gutiérrez out of view. Then he knocked on the barrel and called:

"Here we are! Climb out!"

Ichthyander's head bobbed out of the water and swivelled round. Then he clambered out and sprang down on the ground, his breath fast and strained.

"Thanks a lot, Olsen," he said giving him a firm wet handshake.

"Forget it. Good-bye and be careful. Don't swim too close inshore. Look out for people or you'll get back into jail before you know how."

Even Olsen knew nothing of the instructions Salvator had given Ichthyander.

"Yes, yes," Ichthyander panted heavily.

"I'll swim away, very far away, to quiet coral islands, where ships don't sail. Many thanks, Olsen!" and he ran to the water's edge.

When almost there he turned.

"Olsen! If you ever see Gutiérrez give her my love and tell her I shall remember her all my life!"

And calling, "Farewell, Gutiérrez!" he plunged in.

"Farewell, Ichthyander...." came Gutiérrez's soft response.

The wind had gained in strength and was forcing the man and the girl to bend to resist it. The ocean roared, undertoned by the hiss of sand and the clatter of shingle.

A hand closed on Gutiérrez's arm.

"Let's go, Gutiérrez," came Olsen's gentle command.

He led her onto the road.

Throwing a last glance at the ocean Gutiérrez leaned on Olsen's arm and they headed for the city.

* * *

After serving his term Dr. Salvator returned home and again took up research. At present he's getting ready for a distant journey.

Cristo is still in his service.

Zurita has acquired a new yacht and goes pearling to the Gulf of California. And though he hasn't become the richest man in America he's no cause to complain either. The tips of his moustache, like the needle of a barometer, indicate fair weather.

Gutiérrez has divorced her husband and married Olsen. They live in New York where they work in a cannery.

The "sea-devil" seems to be forgotten on the sea-board of the Rio de la Plata. Only on sultry nights, on hearing some unusual sound in the sea, the older fishermen say to the greenhorns, "That's the way the 'sea-devil' used to blow on his shell," and start a yarn about him.

But there is a man in Buenos Aires who can't forget Ichthyander.

All the urchins of Buenos Aires know the old beggar, the half-wit Indian.

"Here comes the 'sea-devil's' father," they call after him.

But he doesn't pay the slightest attention to them.

Meeting a Spaniard, the old man invariably glares after him, spits on the ground and mutters an oath.

The police leave old Baltasar alone. He is not raving mad, his insanity does no one any harm.

But when a storm starts at sea a strange agitation seizes the old Indian and drives him out of town to the very water's edge where, risking being washed away, he calls, "Ichthyander! Ichthyander!" as long as the storm lasts.

But he gets no answer.

LaVergne, TN USA
02 October 2009
159721LV00001B/12/A